THE LAST WE HEARD OF LEONARD

The Last We Heard of Leonard

Rachel Wyatt

OOLICHAN BOOKS

LANTZVILLE, BRITISH COLUMBIA, CANADA

2002

Canadian Cataloguing in Publication Data

Main entry under title:

Wyatt, Rachel, 1929–

The last we heard of Leonard

ISBN 0-88982-210-7

I. Title.

PS8595.Y3L37 2002   C813'.54   C2002-910282-0

PR9199.3.W88L37 2002

The Canada Council | Le Conseil des Arts
for the Arts | du Canada

We gratefully acknowledge the support of the Canada Council for the Arts for our publishing program.

BRITISH
COLUMBIA
ARTS COUNCIL
Supported by the Province of British Columbia

Grateful acknowledgement is also made to the BC Ministry of Tourism, Small Business and Culture for their financial support.

We acknowledge the financial support of the Government of Canada through the Book Publishing Industry Development Program for our publishing activities.

Published by
Oolichan Books
P.O. Box 10, Lantzville
British Columbia, Canada
V0R 2H0

Printed in Canada

*This book
is dedicated to my dear friend,
the late Urjo Kareda*

Acknowledgements

"Hi! My Name is Harold Fryer" was first published in *The Day Marlene Dietrich Died*. "Pub Lunch" was first published in *Descant*.

I would like to thank Ron smith, Hiro McIlwraith Boga, Linda Martin and Jay Connolly for their consideration and careful editing of the stories in this collection. I am also grateful to some of the "ladies who lunch" with me from time to time and sustain me with conversation and encouragement: Joan Coldwell, P.K. Page, Ann Saddlemyer and Louise Young. And as always, my deep thanks go to Alan for his constant companionship.

CONTENTS

7

TIMBER OF THE GODS

One

But we are doomed, all of us . . . by the immitigable tree which we cannot pass.

—Virginia Woolf, *The Waves*

Yesterday, on the news, there was a picture of a tree full of people. They were sitting in the branches like overripe fruit with water swirling round the trunk below. A woman had given birth to a baby among the leaves. The image had kept Everett awake. He wanted to know what kind of a tree could support so many men and women and a newborn child. None of the reporters had thought to say the tree's name. He supposed he could find it out on the internet but it was surely up to the dispensers of information to tell him.

Everett lives with his wife, Chloe Smith-Pawluck, in a house on a short street in Victoria, British Columbia, Canada. To be precise they live in a wooden-sided house with three bedrooms, one-and-a-half bathrooms, a kitchen, a workroom with Chloe's loom in it, and a large living room with a picture window and a view of the houses across the road. There are three trees in the frame; a Garry oak, a *deodara*, and a Douglas fir. Each one of them grows in the garden of a different house though they were at one time all in the same garden; the property of the big house on the corner which is now ten separate apartments.

Chloe, weaving a pattern of leaves into a wall-hanging for their bedroom, seems to be a happily married woman.

Everett staring out of the picture window at the trees and wondering which would best support a family, is a married man with misgivings. Standing there he pictures himself as a father bending over a crib, looking fondly down at a tiny creature he might have called his own. He pictures himself buried under a fallen fir, bravely smiling as they tell him which of his legs will have to come off. He presses the button on the vacuum cleaner and pushes it to and fro under the window so that Chloe will hear the noise and think he is usefully occupied.

Very soon Chloe and Everett will set out on their Saturday afternoon expedition to fetch groceries.

Everett would rather do the shopping first thing in the morning, at 8 o'clock, say, when the store is nearly empty and the parking lot a paved football field of empty spaces. He would like to do it alone but Chloe says he buys large quantities of everything when it is more economical, shopping for two, to buy small jars, boxes, and packages. That way things don't go bad or get past their use-before date, only to be thrown out. That huge jar of light mayonnaise for example. The exceptions are items like detergent and toilet paper. Besides, she says, and he believes she tells this to her friends, it is a fun thing they can enjoy together.

It is the only thing they do together besides having sex and the enjoyment quotient, for him, is pretty low.

Giving him half the list she will dart off with the cart and after a few minutes of collecting, he will look for her up and down the aisles with his arms full of heavy and awkward objects. He has suggested taking two carts but she seemed to see that as a move towards separate bedrooms. Then with the car trunk laden with paper bags full of supplies for another week, they have this other ritual: coffee and cake.

A breeze is blowing the *deodara's* branches about; now it is a many-armed conductor, leading an orchestra in a sad symphony. Strange foreign tree, its slim trunk curls round and round. When still, its soft branches reach towards the ground as if they want to root themselves independently. He thinks as he drives past it twice a day that it looks like a weary dinosaur.

Coffee and cake. They take turns paying for the little treat. She usually has decaffeinated coffee and a Nanaimo bar. For him it's regular coffee and a butter tart. The tart's sweetness on his tongue reminds him every time of his mother's kitchen; tarts laid out in rows, carrot cakes and loaves of pumpkin bread set on racks to cool. All of it for export. She sold it to one of the bakeries in town. He only got to eat the failures, the tart with the uneven crust, the one with the spilled-over and hardened filling. Chloe has no idea what it means to him to bite into a whole and unblemished tart.

Mary comes out of the house behind the Douglas fir and closes the red door behind her with a bang as if she's quarrelled with Kevin again and will never return.

She is wearing a blue skirt and tweed jacket, going out to meet clients perhaps and sell them a house or a condo by the sea. Everett thinks of running across the road and saying, *Come away with me, we will go to Galiano Island and live on goat cheese and wild herbs and love.* But Mary has got into the car and started the engine and is racing off down the road.

The Douglas fir is a useful tree, a generous tree. Dark green, hung with cones, it gives up its wood to the building of houses for humans.

The *deodara* is a sad tree. A grassier shade of green than the fir, it is a transplant from the Himalayas. It has been modified in its adoptive home and adapted to weep and sometimes to creep. In Hindi, *deodar* means 'timber of the gods.' Everett thought it was called that because its branches were so easily blown about this way and that. That was before he knew that the Hindus used to burn the wood for incense. He still prefers his idea.

This particular specimen has been planted too close to number 1203 and, one of these days, John will have to cut it down with his chainsaw. It sweeps the side of the house as if to remind everyone that it is a living thing too. John told Everett about the incense the last time he and Chloe were asked over there for a drink, nearly two years ago.

Chloe doesn't believe in reciprocal invitations.

In any case, John lives alone and that makes Chloe suspicious. She has an ark mentality and cannot believe that anyone reliable prefers the single life. She imagines dire goings-on after dark when the heavy velvet drapes in John's windows are closed. Her view of the world is clear. Everything seen through a plain uncoloured lens. Everett is an engineer, a man who makes machines work properly. He is excused poetry and visions.

The phone rings.

"I am not answering that," he shouts. But she doesn't hear him so he picks up the phone and says, "Hello," and takes it back to the window as if all kinds of things might happen out there on the street if he turns his back on it.

"We've had to stop the roller."

"We promised them Monday."

"It's the gauge."

"I'll come in later."

"I'm closing up in an hour."

"Come back after dinner. I'll stop by then."

"OK."

Last night at the Home, with all those old worn people sitting around staring, fidgeting, his mother said, "Did any trees blow down? Any big trees blown down, Everett?"

"No, Mom."

She relayed the news to the others.

"No big trees have blown down."

There wasn't a lot of interest.

"No storm, Mom."

"So no big trees blew down?"

"No."

It was as if all the worries of her life had been pressed into that single concern. And if all the trees she'd ever known only remained upright, the world was secure and she would never die. She has forgotten how to bake. He is thankful that she still remembers his name.

"A baby was born in a tree," he said hoping to leave her with a cheerful thought. But she looked at him as if he was an alien bringing news from Mars.

He winds the vacuum cleaner cord round the two hooks and wheels it back to its place under the stairs. How many crumbs and flakes of skin can collect on the floor anyway with both of them out Monday to Friday?

He goes to move the chairs back to their place; two tapestry-covered wing chairs which sit empty most of the time, facing out.

The Garry oak isn't as easily moved as the *deodara* and the Douglas fir. It's a sturdy tree, its branches grow this way and that, sometimes twisting down in a grabby fashion like the trees in the *Snow White* movie that had scared him so much when he saw it with his Dad. The scene in that black forest had driven any heroic thoughts of rescuing young maidens from his mind. At least for a time. His Dad said, "Don't be silly, Ev'ett, they're only trees." Everett was his mother's choice of name and his father always shortened it. She had chosen the formal-sounding Everett to complement the solid Pawluck, thus creating a name suitable for a prime minister, a judge, or a general. When they got married, Chloe added her surname and the hyphen in case of children.

What name did they give to the baby born in a tree?

When it's dark the branches of all the trees on the street

make a sinister pattern. A hero, a knight in shining armour, never appears.

Kevin, Mary's husband, comes out of the house across the road. He closes the door softly, dragging the dog behind him. Hiding his feelings, he walks nonchalantly along the sidewalk. His wife may or may not return to him. She could be making love with a buyer on the floor of an empty house. *A steal at this price, Mr. Jones.* Or she may knock on the door of this house and throw herself into Everett's arms and say, *Take me away from all this.*

The girl who lives in the house behind the Garry oak drives up. She gets out of the car and slams the door with all the force of an insured non-owner. It is her mother's car. The door can fall off for all Elvira cares. She is wearing jeans and a pale blue sweater. She has dropped out of university and is working at his usual gas station. Everett drives fast some days and takes the longer route just so he can use up gas. He hasn't yet got round to siphoning it off in order to make room in the tank for more. The credit-card-in-the-pump system is not appealing to him. He sometimes claims to have left his card at home, and then he goes into the office to pay and tries to make Elvira smile. Elvira wants to be a professional singer but feels the car fumes are destroying her voice.

The oaks are the kind of trees nymphs changed into when gods were importunate. Rejecting Olympian overtures, a girl would suddenly feel her feet rooted into the ground, her body imprisoned in bark and her arms, when she tried to wave a last farewell to her mother, remained bent. Her voice became no more than a sigh.

◆

I am a man, he says to himself, who thinks about machines most of the time. I spend my days in a workshop refining machines, designing better parts for machines. It is my life, I think. I chose to be an engineer because there are no trees left to discover.

Young David Douglas chose to leave his home country and go about the West Coast of Canada identifying plants. His name will remain forever inscribed in books. In his generosity, he dedicated the unusual oak to the Deputy Governor of the Hudson's Bay Company. Was he after Mr. Garry's daughter? Or did he go to him and say, *Sir, you will be forever remembered as a tree with misshapen limbs and leaves that stay on their branches long after they have turned brown?* Was Mr. Garry pleased? Whatever the young botanist's motives or sins, he surely didn't deserve to die in an animal pit, trampled by wild bullocks. But who can ever tell what rewards or punishments are in store? Or whether they will be just or unjust. A man, Everett thought, might just as well believe in fairies as fairness.

Dusting the table top, Everett reckons that he most likely has twenty good years left. Is he prepared to go on being blown about this way and that? A plaything for whimsical gods?

He goes to the door of the workroom and looks in. Chloe is moving the shuttle to and fro in a slow, completely satisfied way, absorbed in the green and blue colours of the yarn as if she is weaving herself into the picture. To and fro. A lovely movement of a woman's arm: The ancient creative gesture.

Mr. and Mrs. Smith, her parents, had died in Florida when violent winds uprooted a palm tree and set it down in the path of their RV. After a fight with her siblings, Chloe was left with enough money to buy the loom and to set aside a few thousand dollars for a trip she plans to take one day. Destination unspecified.

Night after night, his Dad had read to him the long story about the adventurer whose bed was made of a tree and whose wife had stayed at home weaving an endless piece of cloth. *She was faithful, Ev'ett.*

Chloe looks up, sees him and smiles her wide, generous smile. "It's time for our little trip," she says, setting down her shuttle.

He might have said right then, *Go shopping by yourself, Chloe, you don't need me.*

But later, over the rim of his coffee cup, before he bites into one last perfect tart, he has made up his mind to say, *I have to go on a journey, dear. I won't be more than a year or two, perhaps twenty. Keep your eye on the trees. Don't wait up.* He will go and find the name of the tree in which the baby was born. He will go and find his own adventure.

He looks over her shoulder at the pattern she is so carefully making, and there, in the leaves and branches, he sees a face looking out at him. The eyes are evil, the mouth is a grotesque twisted shape. It is the kind of face that could drive a man to run along the path back through the trees as fast as he can towards the light and the safe world he knows. But he remembers what his father told him all those years ago: They are only trees.

NEW LIFE

Everett is looking out the window. He has a pair of binoculars in his hand. The question is, will the sun glint on the lenses and give him away, marking him down as a nosy neighbour? He is innocent of Peeping-Tommery. He's not checking up on John and his new young lover, and if he does catch a glimpse of Elvira it's merely by chance.

He raises the binoculars and looks again at the *deodara* across the road. Twenty feet tall, it has produced its first cone. If not its first, then the first one noticed by John. High up, on one of the smaller branches, the cone, its scales tightly fitting one over another, is a marvel of design. He casts around for something to compare the colour with and can only think of certain kinds of lettuce or peas fresh from the pod. He would have liked a more poetic simile.

John told him that such trees bear cones when they're suffering from stress. It's been a dry summer, and the tree is worried about survival. Around the cone little spots of something glint wet and shiny. Is the tree producing resin to nourish its offspring? Or are those sparkling dots a sign of disease? He opts for the former and sets the binoculars down.

Since the accident he's spent a lot of time looking out, more even than before. He has seen:

Mary leave the house every morning at the same time.

Kevin, now unemployed, take the dog for a walk at a later and later hour each day.

Elvira grow more languid, not even slamming the car door, as if the drought is making a desert of her youth.

John skipping down his driveway and waving his arms with joy when he thinks no one is looking.

In five weeks, lives have moved on while he, Everett, has been stuck here like a branch held fast by a rock in a stream. But he hasn't entirely wasted the time. On the computer, he has designed a cottage in the country for Elvira. It has every kind of labour-saving device and a grand piano. Intertwined E's are carved over the lintel. The door is made of oak. He has also planned his own future, drawn it up like a horoscope, month by month for one year. By then he will be used to living alone and won't need a map.

He has completed, almost, sixteen crossword puzzles, often defeated by musical terms but good at the names of Greek gods and heroes. Thank you, Dad!

He's been able run the shop from home; he's ordered a new lathe, arranged to check the refrigerant coils at the arena, taken on a contract for a custom-built generator. Some evenings John comes round to watch the game with him. Andy drops by after work to discuss the problems he's having with the student they hired to set up a web-site.

He's spent a few hours, mostly at night, asking, Why me? Why now?, and considering who or what was at fault. He has blamed tarts: The sugary surge which came from having two instead of his usual one. It was bargain day at the cafe, a celebration of five years in business.

He also blames the tree stump itself. No more than thirty centimetres high, it was a root left by builders too goddam lazy to blast it out when they extended the parking lot. He shudders as the moment comes back in all its raucous detail. His momentary sense of freedom, his leap of joy and then—cans and apples and frozen vegetables all over the ground, rolling, smashing, bursting. Chloe told him to get up for God's sake and in the next breath yelled at him to stay still. Using her cell-phone, she called for help. The emergency room. Pain. Fear. Sweet sour smell of disinfectant. More pain when Chloe said to the nurse, "He was trying to jump over a root with his arms full of groceries. We all know what he was trying to prove."

He has tried not to blame himself, fearing it will slow down the healing process. It's important for the two ends of bone to knit together peacefully. But he knows it was his desire to fly, to get away, to begin afresh, that brought him down. In the middle of the second butter tart, crunching the pastry, he decided to wait till they got home to tell Chloe he was leaving. If he told her his plans there in the cafe, he reasoned, she might shriek, she might yell out harsh and ridiculous accusations. Or even threats. In public.

After they'd put the groceries away neatly, cold stuff in the fridge, vegetables on the rack, cans on their shelf, that would be the moment. He'd chosen his words with care, framed them in two kindly sentences which left no doors open. An hour or so later he would be on his way to the motel near the shop, his temporary home. He'd tasted that new life along with the raisins and sugar, inhaled it with gasoline fumes as they walked out of the cafe. And had jumped.

The cast is to come off next week.

"Next Monday I'm going to work," he says.

He can hear the vacuum cleaner sucking its way up and down the rug in the hall. He's offered to push it, he could use the machine as a crutch, but Chloe discovered that he wasn't getting into the corners and will do it herself, thank you. He is also excused from the weekly shopping expedition. A man with a cast limping behind her, neighbours asking questions, offering damp sympathy, would be an embarrassment.

So at the moment he's a captive. Chloe has been helpful and kind. She's visited his mother in the Home and has taken time off work to drive him to his physiotherapy sessions. But after her birthday on the 16th, he'll give her that at least, he will speak out. He can't continue to lead this two-stepping life, this odd side-by-side affair of little routines and small expectations. He pictures two horses harnessed to an old-fashioned plough plodding along a never-ending furrow.

He hears her footsteps and turns back to the screen.

News items: Flock of birds fly into jet engine, plane makes unscheduled stop. Mount Etna in eruption. Woman in blue dress peering out at the stream of lava. Floods in Poland. Storm headed to the Gulf Coast. Nature in turmoil.

Chloe comes into the room with the vacuum cleaner and turns it off. Her smile conveys compassion, impatience, and something that makes him hold his breath.

She sits on the edge of the couch and looks at him.

Portentous was the answer to *Weighty—Proust, Ten and Zero*, in the crossword before last.

She adjusts her skirt. It's a much darker green than the cone.

"For a long time," she says, "I've felt a dissonance between us."

It isn't that she's pretentious, she just picks unusual words. Dissonance when distance was what was meant and required. He clings to dissonance and waits.

"Don't give me that look," she says. "I do mean 'want of harmony.' We are not in tune the way we used to be."

He waits again, recalling that *trust and harmony* are written on a monument downtown. He can't remember where it is or who he's meant to trust. And then it comes to him, the words are engraved on a slab of marble outside the police station.

"You see, you have no response," she says.

Music hasn't been one of his hobbies. When he hears Bach, he senses holiness. To Beethoven, he builds towers in his head. But he doesn't know the code and has no idea what to reply to a word like dissonance.

"I've seen you staring out of the window. You look

at that girl, you watch her. It shows that there are lacunae in our lives. And so I have decided."

"What?"

She has a lover. She is going to move in with Kevin after Mary leaves. She's going to do good works in Africa. She's going to use her inheritance to trek across the Mongolian desert with a ski instructor called Fabrice.

"I was going to say something that day and then you fell."

He doesn't hear what she says next because he has begun to laugh. Feeling hysterical, he shouts, "You can't say this. You cannot say this. It's not right. I was going to tell you when we got home. I was about to tell you all of this. These are my words. You can't have my words."

She comes to him and carefully puts her arms round him.

"You do love me," she says. "So you do love me?"

"Oh," he replies, "oh." As if his tongue is on crutches.

"If only you'd said, Everett. If only you hadn't fallen just then. But it can be made right. It can.

"And we'll talk from now on, won't we? We'll try for harmony most of the time."

He throws the binoculars across the room and hops to the door.

"You'll fall," she says.

He turns round and sees that the question is still there between them, a note from her to him. *So you do love me?*

He says, yes. In that moment, he thinks it might be

true. She picks up the binoculars and leads him back to his chair by the window.

"I'll make coffee, honey."

There is one of those silences and then he says,

"Come and see what I've been looking at."

He gives her the glasses although he knows that once he shares it, the cone will lose its magic for him. He tells her to focus on it and asks what the colour reminds her of. He waits.

"It's new life, the green of first things, Everett, the green of regeneration." And she turns to him. "The tree the baby was born in, remember? I think it was a baobab tree."

She's talking about a child.

Pictures flash in rapid succession through his brain: The First Woman reaching out for the Original Apple; his in-laws lying beneath a royal palm; a baby in a tangle of branches; himself tripped by a malicious root. And he knows that what his father told him all those years ago was wrong. Dead wrong. They are not "only" trees.

SYMPOSIUM

Two

I wanna be loved by you

—KALMAR, STOTHART & RUBY 1928,
  FROM *Some Like It Hot*

I gave up long ago trying to get Marilyn out of my mind. An artefact with a husky voice, she was still occasionally whispering to me, hanging about in corners of my life. So when I saw the notice in Friday's paper, I called the bank to say I wasn't well. I accepted Angela's surprise, You're never sick, Cathy, and sympathy, Get better fast, and went downtown. My co-workers would leap to the wrong conclusion: That I was home moping because Yasmin had just left me.

I made my way through the potted palms in the hotel foyer ready to lie to whoever was in charge of the conference: I was a journalist, a member of the committee for culture and tourism, a lawyer from her estate there to protect her rights. As camouflage, I was wearing my only straight skirt and the navy jacket to match with a white turtleneck sweater. My briefcase contained the newspaper and a sourdough loaf I'd bought at the bakery on my way.

Happily, the registration table was deserted. I picked

up a folder and a name tag, wrote my name on a card and slipped it into the plastic cover and pinned it to my lapel. The Crystal Room smelt of stale coffee and air freshener and was only half full. I sat down at the back to read the program. Not a single one of the papers was going to answer my question: What would have become of her if she'd gone on living, if she'd reached old age? It was the question I answered often in my head. In the scenes I created for her, she wore different costumes, different attitudes, and lived out her life against a variety of backdrops. She played to an audience of one.

Polished and brightened by more than the California sun, she had remained with me ever since the day, driving with the family from Montreal to Maine, we saw a placard outside a tabagie: Monroe Dead. Suicide Suspected. I was ten and not sure what suicide was. *Tragic early death. Mystery man seen leaving house.* Suspicion came later. Was it the Kennedys? Had she flown too close to that bright light and fatally singed her wings? Marilyn Moth.

I came to know her intimately. From the movies, from watching videos and reading the books written by people who understood nothing. I knew all about the 'fuzzy end of the lollipop,' from my own life as well as hers. Her lisping voice was released every now and then by an echo of memory, and seemed to call to me from some cloudy set and ask me to invent a future for her.

There are, so far as I know, no Marilyn Anonymous groups.

The professor up there on the stage was talking about

"Monroe's Effect On The Male Psyche." It didn't exactly take an Einstein to figure out that it was profound and that it had to do with fantasy and sex, whether she was waiting at a bus stop, playing a ukelele or standing over a subway grating.

When I was sixteen, my Dad came into my room, turned up his nose at the smell of incense, and asked why I had so many pictures of her on my wall. Why not the Rolling Stones? Why not the Beatles whom he despised as lousy singers with bad haircuts but who were at least male; or, since I was interested in politics, the Prime Minister?

I didn't have an answer.

I do recall that the day we stopped to buy a paper, the day after she died, my Dad was downcast as if he'd lost someone himself. Even my Mom let out a sad sigh and though on the sadness scale it measured no more than her response to mud tracked in on the clean kitchen floor, it made the day significant.

I've imagined Marilyn growing older in many ways. What were her choices as she moved from middle to old age? She would not have become a ninety-year-old recluse photographed sitting in a darkened room as Marlene Dietrich did, a pretty blanket covering her legs to hide the veins as she watched *The Seven Year Itch* for the fiftieth time. *She has worn out seven videos*, her housekeeper, a young man from Idaho, tells the reporter. *She doesn't hear much but when I take her for her daily walk she responds to the smiles of children.*

I caught a cold from the President, she murmurs low in my ear. Her voice is harsher now than when she sang 'Happy Birthday' to him in front of a crowd of high-priced men and women who only wanted to sleep with her. Smoking has damaged her vocal chords. But she whispers to me how, after that song and the cheers that went with it, she followed the chosen guests to the presidential boat but was turned away at the gangplank by the soon-to-be grieving widow. Rejected once again. Not wanted on that voyage.

If she were here now, addressing this group, she might begin, *My last real love*, and then remember that it was her penultimate love. God! *I have been called to my Lord*, she tells the tabloids on her fifty-sixth birthday. The evangelist called her. He calls her his bright shining star and leads her away from a dying career, from glitz and trash, to his own version of the same. He dresses her in white, calls the Hollywood make-up crew to fix her face and hair, and leads her slowly down a curved staircase to the sound of angels singing onto a stage lit with candles and out front into the pure light. Week after week—Omaha, Boise, Buffalo, Toronto—she walks languidly down that staircase. Until one day, lit from inside with gin, falling down the stairs and breaking her leg, she demands her share of the take and limps off to wherever fallen angels go.

The professor was saying, "If we go back to the last half of the twentieth century. We will see the post-war desire for dream and idol. In my book, *A Necessary Camelot*, published last year by Miles and Swann, $18.95, quality paperback, I point out that just as the ice age threw up timely mountains, so does any age produce its icons, its heroes, the ones who suit that particular period. It is mass imagination or, if you will, communal creativity which gives birth to the love-object of the moment." Once again, hardly nuclear physics!

A bossy person got up then as if he had heard enough and announced, "We will now take a fifteen minute break."

Buzzing and humming round the coffee urn and the sticky buns, the scholars tossed clever phrases to one another. I took a bottle of juice from the crate of ice and was followed into a corner by a man with a beard and a briefcase which he held close to him as if it contained a precious relic.

And then this man said, "What's your specialty?"

He meant, what are you doing here? and I wanted to say, *I'm her sister, don't you think we're alike*, and to offer him some hitherto unknown scraps of early biography.

"External Phenomena," I answered, meaning go away and leave me alone.

"Ah yes," he said. He was still young enough to fear seeming ignorant.

"And yours?"

"I'm here as an observer. I teach philosophy of language. I'm interested in the media-driven descriptive style of the fifties and sixties."

"We all have to make a living somehow," I answered, and he laughed a little and told me his name was Irvine Jones.

Of course he had to sit beside me whether he was taken in by my phony answer or not.

"Did you know," he said, "that among those surveyed, more people would prefer Monroe as a dinner companion than Einstein, Shakespeare or any other major figure chosen from the living and the dead. What does this tell you?"

It told me that she is not safe from the prying, the prurient, the pea-brained—people with nothing better to do than think about having dinner with ghosts. But then, who was talking since I'd been living with one for thirty years and more.

When it was time to start again, people shuffled to their seats and a professor from Indiana got up and began by saying how happy he was to be in Canada once more. He'd had the opportunity a few years ago to visit the site of *River of No Return*, and had seen, still hanging there across the Bow River, the box and pulley which the cameraman had used and which no one had bothered to dismantle. He had thrown a lily into the water in her memory.

I tuned out when he said, "Like Alexander, she died in a timely moment."

Why? I wanted to shout. Was she irredeemable?

In her sixties, she comes out onto a real stage, tights covering the still perfect legs, and declaims Hamlet's soliloquy. The applause nearly takes the roof off the Lincoln Centre. By then she has become the great actress she always wanted to be. Her Gertrude, world-renowned, makes absolute sense of the prince's oedipal gestures. Medea in Greece. Hedda in Oslo. Marilyn Triumphant.

My Mom used to say she was no better than she ought to be, a phrase I never understood. She wanted to wall-paper over my posters. "That woman is not someone to imitate," Mom said. As if, with my looks and straight legs, I could become the idol of millions as a matter of choice.

The scholar on the platform said, "The Monroe Doctrine." The conferees around me sniggered.

"I should say," he went on, pleased with his little joke, "'syndrome' or perhaps 'equation.' Beautiful equals bad equals deserving of, shall we say, death, shall we say, being unloved?"

For heavens sake!

What would *she* have been like as a scholar? She could have been a lot smarter than these dummies who were using her as a stepping stone to some higher shelf in academia. Looking through tortoiseshell-rimmed spectacles, her grey hair swept tightly back, she lectures on the use of music in film. Showing clips of *Some Like it Hot*, she teaches young actors how to move while playing small stringed instruments.

Had DiMaggio been a less jealous husband, she could have moved into the lovely obscurity of home, children, and local theatre. He died last week thinking he was going to see her again. Look out, Marilyn!

She called to me yesterday, her voice sexy and persuasive, saying, "I had so much to live for." She couldn't know that Yasmin, whose legs were as near perfect as hers, had left me, left the office, left town as if pursued down a narrow alley by fire trucks. All I had done was ask her to move in with me permanently.

Marilyn knew what it was to be stranded by the highway. But our relationship, Marilyn's and mine, was one-way only. She had no advice to offer and couldn't sympathise with me in my loneliness.

Would you trade those few glamorous years for thirty-eight more years of obscurity? I would ask her at the phantom dinner, knowing full well what her answer might be.

The bearded professor leaned over and said into my ear, "My room number is 413."

"Thirteen isn't your lucky number," I whispered back.

Her suburban home, continuing the baseball marriage, is full of laughter. She swings her toddler round holding his hands and promises never to abandon him. Joe is in the garage carving a small bat for their son, making sure it is curved correctly as he smooths away the rough places.

Yasmin accused me, while she gathered up her discs and bonsai garden and scented candles and the housecoat she kept at my place, of only ever giving her half my attention.

"I would like to suggest," the man on the stage was saying, "that had Arthur Miller not married her, he would have written at least two more major plays. Time was taken up stroking her thighs which might have been used more creatively. Feeling his way where others had felt before, he felt old. But he worshipped her for a time, his golden goddess, his own perfect girl, his Marilyn, ignoring the first commandment. Had this

woman not thrown herself in his path or had she been
able to tend to him as a wife—I'm being ironic here—
both their lives would have been different and she
might be with us here today. What I'm truly saying is
that these two clashed like asteroids but it was a
marriage made in heaven for the short-term only. It
was not meant to last."

Miller in old age, senility brought on early by too
much fucking, is being pushed in his wheelchair by
the actress who is no longer glamorous but has achieved
a saintly look through her selfless devotion to the
tiresome old invalid. It was noted that she kept her
legs covered during this period of her life.

A stern woman, blonde, sharp-featured, in a black
and pink suit, snapped, "Can we truly say she is an
icon for our time?" I wondered if she was into bondage.
And she went on, "If we think of film and television,
we are bound to think of Plato's cave."

Oh sure! We talk about it at the office all the time
between arranging a mortgage for Ms. Pasemko,
refusing a loan for Mr. Brown's opportunity-of-a-
lifetime in ladieswear, and deciding whose turn it is to
get the coffee.

But after all, I thought, at least these people are
considering the life of a woman they had never known.
They might have set her on a very different pedestal
from mine. For me she was a companion, a person I
could have loved. For them she was someone to be
seriously studied against a background of time and
ideas. I looked round at them all more kindly. And
although I certainly wouldn't go to his room, I decided
to have a drink with Irvine later, just to be friendly

and to put off the moment of returning to my empty space. I try not to reject people, even in my own worst moments of rejection.

There was a silence, the hush of expectation. The speaker pushed the lectern to the back of the stage. Familiar music filtered in through loudspeakers. This had to be the tribute mentioned in the program as the last item before lunch.

And then a man came from the wings holding hands with another who was holding hands with another, eight of them in a chain up there on the platform. All of them wearing blonde wigs and dresses like the *Seven-Year-Itch* dress. A wind machine blew air at them as they pranced across the stage, showing their thick hairy legs. It was a frightening, multiplied image as they put their hands down to hold their skirts in place, a truly horrible travesty.

She didn't expect the best, Marilyn, didn't expect people to reach out to her warmly and with love always but when they did, she believed them. She trusted them. Marilyn Deceived.

This was meant to be a serious conference. But they were like all the rest. They couldn't, even for only two whole days, take her seriously. Forty-eight hours! Everybody was laughing. All these clever, ugly people showing their capped teeth, their gold molars, saliva on their tongues, were laughing. And faintly, from a very long way off, I could hear Marilyn saying, *Why are they doing this?*

"I thought we might sit next to each other at the

banquet," Professor Jones said to me when he'd caught his breath, when he'd stopped banging his hands together in applause, while I let all of Marilyn's future lives fade to black.

"I haven't got a ticket," I said and as I stood up to leave, I kicked him sharply on the ankle.

He would never understand why.

BALLOON EXIT

Three

It's easy enough to get actors on to the stage. Getting them off is quite another matter.

—THEATRE DIRECTOR

"I once played the part of Natasha. Natasha from *War and Peace*." Too late, he realises he has spoken the words aloud.

"Don't be ridiculous, you're five foot ten and you've got big feet and, let's not forget, you're a man."

"Not everything happens on stage, Mattie."

"So what then?"

"Nothing."

We were in love. She went away on tour. It was a make or break offer. A real stepping stone. She couldn't refuse. We wanted to get married right then. Her mother insisted on us waiting till she came back.

"Once again, you've got big feet."

She was nineteen. I was twenty-five. As soon as I saw her I knew she was the one.

They are sitting on the balcony of Actors Offstage. It's a cool day for June but they prefer the outside to the lounge. He's rocking to and fro and she's in a basket chair with cushions around her, bright cushions in vivid tearing blues and greens. Above them hang baskets of geraniums, the red and pink colours of blood. On most mornings they play their what-were-your-favourite-roles? game, offer each other a few overripe quotations, and move into silence. But today there is another drama going on and they are secretly glad that neither of them has been invited to read for the main part. Their time will come soon enough, ready or not.

"It can't be long till lunchtime."

"When she came on, she lit the place up."

"We were all lit up when we moved into the spot."

"She didn't need a spot."

He takes out his handkerchief, gift of the daughter who still comes to visit now and then. To the other one, the one he first met when she was five and who'd learnt by then to think of him as an absconder, he writes letters twice a year and jokingly signs himself King Lear. Did Lear have another name? Like Edward or Ethelbight or Charles? He pretends to blow his nose so that he can dab his eyes.

She taps his arm, another light gone on over her brain.

"You don't mean you and her? You and Hermione!"

"That wasn't her name when I knew her first."

"You're going to tell me, aren't you?"

"Do you want me to?"

"Yes."

He closes his lips tight lest words escape him against his will. If she'd said no, he might have gone on and told her the sadness of his life which he has never told anyone and especially not her. But she is waiting, ears open, and he would have to say it loudly because she's getting deaf and God knows how many others are lurking nearby, waiting for him to spill it all out.

"I heard the old stories. Everybody said there was something. I never believed it. She was too grand for you, for all of us."

"I have to go."

"They won't let you in."

"To the bathroom!"

He puts his feet forward firmly on to the wooden slats of the deck, and presses down, pushing with his hands on the arms of the chair. That way he can stand up without seeming to stagger and with a minimum of pain.

He hears Mattie whispering, "You and Hermione."

Mattie is a tired old woman now, full of wrinkles and broken memory. She eats only soft food and spills a good deal of it. She once had amazed audiences in small towns with her unusual interpretations of various classical roles. Her Andromache, in the days when people knew who Andromache was, earned her rave notices in local newspapers.

"Hermione and you? Ridiculous!"

He pretends not to hear and goes inside and takes the elevator to the fourth floor. Harriet Smithers who became Hermione Heath between Toronto and Stratford in Spring 1954, is lying inside room 412. There is a peephole in the door but no way of seeing in from the outside.

He pushes the door lightly. No busybody nurse is sitting there. They've carelessly left her alone with a temporary drip in her arm. In moments the ambulance will be here to fetch her away. It will carry her screaming through the streets of the city, a dramatic way to go but not her way.

He sits by the bed and holds her hand.

"In the tent, remember," he says, leading her back.

Is that you my love, my Antony, my faithless one?

I am dying, Egypt, dying.

"Shakespeare in the Park. Hot summer night. You were wearing a pink gauzy costume for Titania. And not much else."

On such a night as that, had Hermione and he become one under the stars.

"Next day, you took me home with you. Your mother screamed and threw a vase of flowers at me yelling, 'He is nobody. He will hold you back!'

"Then she brought out a weird kind of First Aid box and dabbed something on the cut. Said she was sorry, she had never been violent like that before but you were her only daughter, Harriet. And you were going to be a star. And you said, 'I love him, Mom. Leave him alone.'

"We both cried."

♦

Then Mrs. Smithers had said, "All right, call yourselves engaged if you must. But you don't get married till Harriet gets back from New York."

Did Harriet's mother smile then? A mean, disbelieving sort of look? As if she was thinking, he's young, he'll never last a whole year? A look like that is fixed in his memory: a malevolent Cheshire Cat grin.

"Next morning, we went out and climbed to the top of the hill, Hermione, and watched balloonists drifting down to earth. You preferred, you said, balloons that went up. And we laughed at the play we'd both acted in, a new play by a young author who didn't know how to get his characters off the stage. There was the heroine (you) in the desert, standing there, her lover (me), dead, and a balloon drops a rope and lifts her (you), dangling into the wings and out of sight. Blackout. Corpse (me), quietly gets up and exits to return for curtain call, miraculously alive.

"We made love on the hill, we made love that night in bed, we made love on the floor. We were nearly late for next day's rehearsal."

He rummages round in the bedside drawer to see if she's kept the ring she threw at him and which he had thrown back shouting, "It didn't mean anything."

Every day now for a week, he's come to see her and talk to her. There've been no answers. She moved into the Home a year ago and scarcely seemed to recognise him. Kept to herself, locked inside her own head, whispering to no one in particular. Occasionally, entering the dining room, she had stopped in the doorway and waited for applause and sometimes the others had responded to her cue. She would then take her bow and move towards a table by the window. She still loved light.

The year passed. My betrothed came towards me.

"You never gave me a chance to tell you. I'm going to tell you now." He put his mouth close to her ear. "It was when I was in Bala. Couldn't resist the offer. There were six weeks left of that awful year. You were coming back. I only had to wait another forty days and forty nights. I'd already waited three hundred and twenty-five. With, you know, a little bit of comfort here and there. Nothing serious. Always thinking of you. Only you."

But some offers are meant to be resisted.

"And then. Call it lust, call it extreme sexual arousal but it was only a moment. Only a night. It meant nothing! 'What a liar!' I can still hear you saying that, my love. *My betrothed came towards me with daggers in her eyes.*

"How did your mother find out? Were you ever happy

with that boring one-note fellow you finally married. He couldn't act his way out of a paper bag."

Her eyes flick open for a second.

"In that long year, you were at the acting school meeting famous people. You sent me postcards of the Empire State Building, the Statue of Liberty, saying you missed me. One from Staten Island saying you wished so much I was there.

"I was in repertory in Ottawa doing *Private Lives* and a warped adaptation of Shakespeare. I had the worst cast Lady M. you could imagine. Shrill and mean and couldn't have driven a man to the nearest McDonald's let alone to murder. I tried to ignore her but on stage she was all over me, breathing in my ear when she got the chance. You're so sexy. The director, it was Brian, remember him? Hopeless. He shouted at her and told her to smarten up. She turned up in my room in tears. Your postcards, tacked to the wall, should have stopped me. Was it the ill luck of the Scottish Play? Another curse?

"Our life together, yours and mine, was going to be so good. The setting: An old stone house outside Toronto. There together in the off-season, we would plant a garden. We'd grow berries. Make jam. Have little parties. Play all the main parts: Equal, line for line. Large hat, flowery gown for you. Neat slacks, white shirt, maybe a cravat for me. Passion and Domestic Bliss. Starring opposite each other in life and in make-believe. Like Tandy and Cronyn.

"She was all over me. I couldn't stop her."

◆

He can't help crying. He hates this old-age weakness that makes his eyes water at the least thing. He knows he has 'rheumy' eyes.

Hermione shifts slightly under the sheet and her eyes open and close again. He has to move quickly on to the next act.

"You returned on a Friday. I couldn't get away till the Sunday. But then, carrying the biggest bunch of carnations you've ever seen, I knocked on the door of your house. I could hear your mother's voice: *He's done it once. He'll do it again. He will betray you.* You came to the door and opened it only to slam it in my face. After you'd said those cruel words.

"Six months later, I was Richard the Third in Saskatoon. She was pregnant and blamed me. I ran. I sent you a letter from Whitehorse, pleading with you to let me in out of the cold. I kept on running. And then. And then.

"Next time I saw you, you were in Stratford, you had become Hermione, a star, a diva. The star who could and did make demands. Through the years, we wrote postcards, made jokes about 'balloon exits' and every time I saw you, I wanted to have that day back, to start over.

"Five years after that she turned up with the child. The child smiled at me. Just about the only time. You wrote to congratulate me on my marriage. I settled down to domestic bliss.

"And so, dear love, we all ended up here together. What mattered?"

◆

He lies beside her and she is smiling, forgiving him, loving him. Something in her head shifts. Now she is looking at him, imploring. *Don't let them torture me.*

He nudges the drip in her arm and the needle slips away from the thin yellow skin. He pats her head, strokes her hair, moves her arm to make it look as though she has shaken the needle loose. She lets out a swooshing sigh that is like air let out of a balloon.

He goes as quickly as he can out of the room. The nurse is returning but sees only a shambling old man. He reaches the elevator, innocent.

The ambulance is coming up the driveway. Hermione will very soon be gone.

He stands still for a moment looking over rows and rows of heads to the lighted Exit signs beyond. There is no applause.

"How is she?" Mattie asks.

"She's sleeping peacefully," he says.

"We should all be so lucky," she replies. "So now you can tell me?"

He lowers himself gingerly into the rocker.

"Her mother very much wanted us to get married," he begins. "Came after me, cajoled. All that. But I could see Harriet/Hermione was on her way up. Very much a career woman. Marriage at that time would have been a drag for her. Children would have held her back."

She leans over and pats his cheek. He can see the soup stains on her sweater.

"Well that left you free for me, sweetheart." She adjusts her cushions and looks at him, something of that simpering Lady Macbeth in her still.

"Yes," he answers, seeing her dimly against the backdrop of bloody colours. "I guess it did."

"And you know, darling, Natasha might not have been happy with Prince Andrei."

There! It is said. A lie. A downright terrible lie. A lie that is quite possibly true and which breaks his heart all over again.

Life is a narrowing down, a dwindling of options. His last role, the aged retainer in a critically misunderstood production of *The Cherry Orchard*, had ended in a quiet sleep.

He turns to her and says with some of that gallantry which had made him briefly famous, "Whereas with you, my love."

"I was the understudy," she says, as if she has known that all along.

He can hear the ambulance men opening doors.

He knows Mattie was the one who made the call to Mrs. Smithers all those years ago. If he were to get up and try to hit her, he would most likely fall into her lap. There is nothing for it but to wait for a balloon to come and lift him up and away.

"I can hear the bell," she says.

He gets up painfully to go inside, and hopes there will be lemon pie for dessert.

ONE MINUTE WE WERE DANCING

Four

"Everything's done by machines nowadays"
"Not everything, mother."

—OVERHEARD ON A BUS

Ruth was glad she was still able to balance on one leg and rest her foot on the bathroom counter. The phone rang while she was considering that the hairs were fewer now and took longer to grow back. She lifted her leg down and hopped into the bedroom to pick up the receiver before her own detached voice could tell the caller she was either on the other line or unable to come to the phone at this time.

"What are you doing right now?" A purred question from a stranger.

"Shaving my legs," she replied. "And I'm wearing . . . "

The man hung up.

Driving to work, trying to call his loved one on the cell phone for a little remote sex en route, one wrong digit had led him astray. Whispered romance. Where now the love notes of yesteryear?

When she was young, Ruth had rubbed her legs smooth with a sandpaper mitt in case she met a boy who wanted to run his hands all the way up her thighs.

Now she shaved so that hairs wouldn't show through her sheer lime green pantyhose. She put the LadySharpe back in its little case and considered the expense and pain of wax.

"I am not," she said aloud to the parrot Jim had given her to keep her company when he left, "going to think about the gulf of years between sandpaper and a cordless razor."

Like an ice crevasse, that gulf was miles deep and hard to climb out of once you were in it.

Being a creature of cloth and wire, the parrot said nothing.

Mind back to the present. What to wear for a last day? Fashion writers take note: Microfibre suit in dark pink. Shirt, green. Hair the responsibility of Daryl at Cutting Edge. Shoes new, pinching at the big toe slightly but smart.

The coffee pot was squeaking like an ill-treated child. The safety feature which was supposed to stop it from turning itself on when there was no water in it had failed again. She unplugged it and looked for the jar of instant she kept in the fridge.

The letter on the kitchen counter wasn't a love note, only a reminder of love. It had knocked Ruth's mind off centre. When she read it, she hadn't run amok, cried, laughed, gone into hysterics; the weight of memory had held her still. But his face, his accent, her sudden onset of passion and the green hedgerow that turned red overnight came into her memory as clear as yesterday's dinner.

And in Belfast, the lawyer who had signed the letter hoped she would reply at her earliest convenience. How many, late on in life, got a summons from the past like this? Where could she turn for advice? No one had understood at the time. Why would they now? The letter might as well have been shrieking aloud, *Answer me! Say something!*

But first she had to deal with today. End of the world as she'd known it. Long-dreaded moment. *Aren't you lucky. Now you'll be able to . . .* Kind well-wishers always finished that sentence according to their own desires.

At the office, little gifts and cards would lie on her desk. *We'll miss you. Keep in touch.* What vile words those were. Keep in touch! Hollow command that let the speaker off the hook: It's your responsibility to keep this wonderful relationship going, you won't ever hear from me.

"You saw that movie. Didn't you think it was the perfect expression of first love?" Daryl said, taking the rollers from her hair, running the shaver up her neck. "What do you think of the colour?"

He didn't notice the sudden tears in her eyes and couldn't have imagined her as a girl, sand-papered legs encased in slacks, cycling along a country road between damp fields on a day that was the best and worst of her life.

"It's very red."

"Sunset glow. Perfect with that green blouse."

On any normal morning, she would by now have read several chapters of the latest offering, attended a meeting to select the next six titles, argued with Elise about semi-colons and talked on the phone to another hopeful author. *What we look for at Marchant is romance with difficulty.*

She walked down the avenue aware of her own bright image, attracting looks that were most likely as much surprise as admiration. Even the woman scrubbing the winter grime off the blue tiles in the fountain leaned on her long-handled brush to stare. So they were expecting summer to come again. Water to flow. There would be pansies and impatiens on the island in the centre of this busy road before long. And not a soul would notice that she, Ruth McLennan, walked there no more.

She traced the streets in ever-decreasing rectangles till she reached the twenty-storey building on Berton. Here she had laboured for three decades. A labour, they always joked, of love. Love's labour sometimes lost. Easier to lose now that manuscripts arrived on small discs. Brick-sized envelopes were going the way of heroes who could do no wrong.

"No, it's not because I haven't mastered the new software," she'd said to her sceptical sister on the phone. "I'm retiring from choice."

Even as a girl she'd lied easily.

She rode up in the elevator with two well-dressed men. They grinned at each other over her head and silently slotted her into the Marchant file. Seventeenth floor. Where the crazy people spent their days in useless fantasy.

Poor things, businessmen, Ruth thought in response. Always in uniform, always the same, the shirt, the suit grey or black or navy. It had to do something to their minds. Picking out a tie every morning was their one chance of self-expression.

Balloons were stuck to the office walls. Some had printed messages on them. She didn't dare to look. *I am about to scream. It is too soon.* Was that the girl talking to the wounded man, or the older woman talking to her boss? *I have life left in me yet.* Sweet Alexander telling his own lie as he lay there bleeding?

"Not a word, Elise," she said. "I know I'm too early." She slipped into her own but no-longer-her-own office for one last hour. An angel flew across the computer screen folding her icy wings. Ruth tapped in her code and the dreaded words appeared, 'Password not recognised.' She was already locked out of the system. Left for dead by the side of the highway; cyber-roadkill.

Outside the real window, winter was shaking down its last flakes of snow. She sat staring at them, thinking scattered thoughts of green fields, of a brief dream, of her reply to the lawyer's letter. To accept that bequest would be to take a leap into the dark, backwards and with her eyes closed. A cordless bungee jump. Once there, the past would rise up to meet her. Could she bear it?

Pierre came up behind her and put his hands on her shoulders and said, "Y'know, Ruth. I once thought we might've."

"But we didn't."

"Never too late?"

"Much too late."

"What are you going to do now?"

"I'm not sure."

"Don't despair."

"I have plans to do just that."

Despair after all was part of the Marchant stock-in-trade. How could there be rescue and recovery without it? Where was romance if lovers were never in distress? And what chance was there of the real thing here? All possible dialogue between two lovers was either lying round the office in hard copy or staring at them from small screens.

Pierre was a handsome man, grey-haired now. It was hard to remember why they hadn't rushed into bed except that he was married at the time and she knew his wife.

He called out, "Come on everyone. Party time!"

To her, he said, "They'll expect a few words."

The speech she wanted to make began: Once a long time ago I visited a place where people were killed on a regular basis, and in a cosy white-washed cottage, there was a grandfather clock which kept perfect time.

"OK," she answered, "when we've had a drink or two."

Pierre was fussy about wine and there would be only good white and the Chilean red he kept saying was the best for the price.

Elise handed round a plate of smoked salmon rolls and Bertie had set out enough sushi for fifty people. Ruth wanted nothing so much as a large piece of the angel cake with lemon filling that her mother had made every birthday. Mother, beating the egg whites by hand with a wire whisk walking about the kitchen with the bowl tucked in the crook of her arm, had thrown her daughter life lines: "Don't be too eager, Ruth." "There are lots of fish in the sea." "You'll know the right man when you meet him."

The right man was shot, mother, and his blood was the colour of your raspberry jam.

Mother and father had walked, it always seemed, side by side, slept side by side like a knight and his lady on an old stone tomb. *My father was proud when I got this job.*

She looked round at this 'family,' the employees of the Toronto branch of Marchant Romance. Fifteen of them worked to produce books that people read on subway trains to pass the time; stories that opened doors into lush gardens, to passion on sandy shores and to self-sacrifice without lasting bitterness.

Kim stepped forward. Holding up her glass, she said, "To Ruth! Forgetting the time she erased *A Cowboy's Heart.*"

Laughter. And then Marion, chic in a fine wool dress, said, "But remembering her devotion to the text."

How about remembering maybe that I brought in Beauty's Fall? *And the handsome author with it.*

Not many men in this field: An image of a green meadow filled with women and one man among them standing out like a dark presence.

"I am going to dedicate my next book to you, Ruth," he had said one day.

He never did because by the time he'd got to page eighty-three, he'd moved on, tired of her nightmares.

By then her mother was saying, "Don't be too fussy, Ruth. A woman past forty . . . "

My true love was my cousin once removed and he died in a war that never ends.

"There have been huge changes in technology in my lifetime," she heard herself saying. "My bicycle had only three gears."

My aunt had baked a fruit cake for my sixteenth birthday but I was too excited to eat.

We're going to a dance tonight, my cousin Alec said.

How lovely, the girl Ruth might have replied but had more likely said, *smashing* or whatever the wow-word was in 1945.

"I've been looking forward to this day for thirty years. Seriously, it's been great working with you all."

And oh that Irish cousin, the face, the accent, the dark hair, the dark eyes. She had travelled to Clanagh that October bathed in the wonderful feeling that peace had come and with it the freedom to travel again and to fall in love.

"Loaded for bear, Ruth!" Bertie said, looking at her clothes, her hair. "Going out with a bang?"

"If only!"

"A flash then."

"And outside in a carriage, her secret lover waits to take her home to his castle."

Smiling at her, radiating kind feelings, they would have laughed at the thought of old Ruth dancing a jig, gazing moon-eyed at her cousin. Marchant guidelines forbade girls to find the love of their lives at sixteen.

On the night of the dance, the soldiers guarding the

door of the village hall in that little Irish town were no surprise. There had been soldiers everywhere all the time for five years of war.

"So tell us, Ruth. What's it going to be? Europe? A quick climb up Everest?"

I plan to sit in the privacy of my apartment, listening to the recorded voices of friends: Answer the phone, Ruth, I know you're there. Have you forgotten what day it is?

The rays from the microwave oven will strike at my hands, and I will eat fragments of stale bread and cheese and suffer from diverticulitis.

Pierre beckoned to her. He was holding a parcel in his hand. "We'd like to give you this special token of . . . "

"A book token," someone shrieked.

"A token of his undying love!"

"Shall I open it now?"

"Yesyesyes."

She felt the shape of the package and took the silver wrapping paper off slowly.

The vase was a copy of a Greek urn. It was truly beautiful but she couldn't prevent herself from thinking of ashes.

"If you want to change it."

"I love it."

In relief, round the vase, warriors pursued young women they could never catch.

Heroes had changed in her thirty years of work. Women had careers and no longer gave them up or leapt with joy because some dark stranger held out his hand and offered a lifetime of drudgery in exchange for sex and financial support.

I have remained single from choice. I have remained single because the girl with the clean-shaven legs didn't listen to her mother and fell in love with the dark stranger.

Phrases and shards of laughter were floating about her.

"You believe that cover!"

"Bright hearts hung on branches!"

"Smartie-coloured hearts. Like a fucking shoe tree."

"Or P.D.James."

Hearing them, Ruth knew she was fading, becoming a dim image on the office screen.

That May in England there was dancing in the streets. The windows of all the houses were uncovered to let light out and in. And she had sailed across the narrow water to Ireland, a carefree girl.

It took that girl an hour or more to dry her long hair by the fire. What wouldn't she have given for a hair dryer? And all the while he was waiting, waiting.

Alec came to her and said, "Dance with me, little cousin."

It wasn't easy because that was no waltz, no military two-step or simple polka. It was a hopping, high-stepping dance she'd never danced before. She traced his initials with her finger on the back of his jacket while they hopped and leapt round the room until . . . it took a deep breath even now for her to get past that 'until.'

Dear Ms. McLennan, We are writing to inform you that Katie Olsen who died on December 19th, last year, in Sydney, Australia, has bequeathed the property, Stone Cottage, The Lane, Clanagh, to you in her will. Please accept our apology for taking so long to contact you. We had difficulty in tracing you. The cottage is at the moment empty and we are anxious to know your instructions, at your earliest convenience.

"She's miles away. Come back to us, Ruth."

"Tell us the best times, Ruth. The good times."

I grew up in a city drab with wartime restrictions. How could I not think I had come to an enchanted fairyland that Irish October morning? It was a village in County Down with whitewashed houses and doors that closed in two halves. The bottom half kept out the chickens that wandered up and down the street.

She glanced round at their faces. Marge, Wayne and Gina who were young, discounted her. Pierre was on his way out too. Bertie and Charlene looked at her with pity because she was leaving the world of romance forever.

"You want to take a few balloons home, Ruth?"

Well, why not. I will walk along the street with them tied to my wrist.

"I'll miss you all," she said.

Young Ruth had travelled north from Leeds on a train to Scotland and then on a boat across the Irish Sea. Old Ruth would fly from Toronto to Belfast in the time it had taken her then, in 1945, to go from Leeds to Stranraer by train and then by boat to Larne. The lawyer's phone number was on the letterhead.

"Are you going to write a book, Ruth?"

There was even louder laughter. It was a standing joke. Everybody who left the company was going to write a memoir: *Writers I have known.*

"Of course," she said.

Their laughter followed her out into the hall. They would all go back to work, a little intoxicated. Back to their romantic dilemmas.

The woman with the long brush was gone from the fountain and two men were filling it with water. Ruth sat down on the bench beside the war memorial and dictated the first few words of the book into her recorder. "One minute we were dancing a jig."

One minute we were dancing. A black and fearful moment later she was in the car driven by Katie. Alec lay in the back, bleeding. The two men who came into that village hall were wearing masks. They never spoke. Were never caught. Never, apparently, pursued.

The story was too violent for Marchant Incorporated. It wasn't fiction. But it was romance. It was mad tragedy. It wasn't an appealing story but it was the only story she had ever wanted to tell.

UNACCEPTABLE

BEHAVIOUR

The music of Schumann gave way to a voice with a lyrical accent, much too lyrical to be saying, "Today in Belfast, sixteen men were shot . . . "

Ruth took her hand out from behind the grandfather clock and caught her ring on the wallpaper. She tried not to tear another strip loose. Tenants had come and gone, had decorated the cottage top to bottom, but none of them had ever moved the clock. They had simply gone on tucking the edges of the new paper in behind the walnut case.

She moved nearer to the radio and sat down. After the headlines, the news would be read out in full, the whole story told. The old clock would wait. After all, in the forty-six years since she'd stood in front of it with Alec, it had neither stopped nor lost time.

"In London the Prime Minister said," the voice continued, "that this tragic story once more high-lights . . . "

Sixteen young men lay in hospital, and their wives

sitting by them knew there would be no more dances for them, no real work, ever again.

The window cleaner out there, a young fellow with dark hair and blue eyes, smiled in at her and went on rubbing the glass for all he was worth. Then he moved on and let the soapy water run in little streams down another pane.

Another letter from Pierre in Toronto reminded her that her friends thought she was out of her mind. In the sympathetic words used for invalids, he'd asked how she was feeling. And then how she was getting on with writing her memoirs.

She wasn't going to admit that she was homesick for busy streets and cafes, or that the damp wasn't helping her arthritis. As for her memoirs, she told him she was already at page fifty-three and would soon send him the manuscript.

That lie would keep him quiet for a while. The truth was that the very smells and sounds of this little town kept one reel of memories going round in her mind like a horse on carousel. It began with the sea.

October 1945. A short school holiday. Ruth stood on the deck of the ferry, crossing the North Channel from Stranraer to Larne. The boat was full of soldiers going home at last, six months after the war had ended in Europe. Some of them were singing while others quietly watched for the first sight of the Irish coast. Ruth stayed back trying to ignore the heaving of the deck as it swayed from side to side. She was feeling faint when a soldier touched her and offered her water in a tin cup.

"This is where the seven seas meet," he said. "It's always rough."

Had he really put his arm round her and did she lean on him, her face against the damp wool of his uniform? She did remember asking him where he'd fought. He'd talked about Italy as if he and his friends had been on a picnic, a long exciting jaunt, and had the time of their lives.

"Patrick Monaghan at your service," he said.

She told him her name and that she was going to Clanagh because her uncle and his family, bombed out of their Belfast home, had moved there. He laughed. His brother lived in Clanagh.

"There's to be a party for me there on Saturday," he said.

And she had thought, this is the first time I've travelled so far alone, and here I am having an adventure. Something to tell the girls at school when she got home.

"I have to go to Belfast to get demobbed," Patrick Monaghan told her. "I'll write to you." And he copied her address from the label on her suitcase.

The soldiers cheered as the boat approached the docks. Patrick Monaghan said he would see her to the train but would then have to travel with his group. He kissed her on the cheek and Ruth felt as if peace had made everything possible. And there was a future for romance.

A few hours later she was inside a white-washed cottage that smelled richly of bacon, of cheese, of butter, of chocolate. Her Aunt Hilda was gripping her arm like the witch in *Hansel and Gretel* and saying to Uncle Brian, "Here she is, the starved-looking wee thing. Five years of nothing to eat."

Her bedroom under the thatched roof had flowered curtains at the window, a soft bed with a crazy quilt over it, and a plate of biscuits on the dresser in case she should wake up hungry.

She didn't mention the soldier on the boat but two days later the postcard arrived. Her Uncle picked it up and his face darkened as he looked at it.

"You'll not be meeting him!"

Uncle's hair was untidy, as black as her father's but allowed to grow thick and unruly. There was a fierceness in him that his brother had lost in his years in England.

"He's a Roman Catholic, Ruth. Could you not see? A Catholic! Have you no idea what that means?"

"I'm not planning to marry him," she said but knew at once that she should have kept quiet.

Uncle hadn't finished. "They get you into their clutches. All they want is to breed and cover this place with their own. To drive us out. After these centuries, they want the whole country and they'll do anything at all to get it. We do not talk to them."

That May, in England, flags as big as blankets had appeared like magic hanging from windows. Endless snaking lines of people had danced through the streets singing and yelling. Anyone who could play an instrument was out there adding to the sound: a great cacophony of peace.

"He was kind to me," she said.

"They are the enemy," Uncle shouted.

♦

Penny, Hilda's niece, arrived from Belfast to stay for the weekend. Seventeen, small and quick, laughing at Ruth's accent, she was there to be company for her. They might have gone to the pictures, she said, but THEY had tried to burn the picture house down.

"They invaded?" Ruth asked, imagining soldiers in jackboots stomping up and down this little street.

"No, I don't mean the Germans, silly," Penny replied.

And what was Ruth going to wear to the dance, the box supper? What did she have? Her pink dress would do. Would her mother mind if Penny cut some of the lacy stuff off? Ruth answered, "Not at all."

She borrowed Uncle's bicycle and rode with Penny to fetch two dozen eggs from a farm which belonged to distant relatives. As they rode between yellowing hedgerows, Penny explained about the box supper.

"You take a little box, put in some sandwiches, cake, scones if you like. And decorate the outside of it. The men bid for them and you dance with whoever buys yours."

Then Penny told her to expect some sadness in the farmhouse. Alec and Katie's mother had died a couple of years ago.

Katie was in the kitchen turning triangles of soda bread on a black griddle for the workers' morning tea. Her arms and face were as red as beetroot.

"Welcome," she said. "Come in."

Ruth was sitting by the fire eating her own piece of

fresh bread with butter and jam on it when she first saw him.

Katie cried out, "Alec, here's another cousin for you, all the way from England. And thin from eating nothing but wee bits of this and that."

Alec said nothing but took notice all the same. Ruth was struck by the poetic look in his eyes, and yet there was a boldness about him as if he would have made a good soldier. He had most likely been exempt from the army against his will: Farming was work of national importance.

Katie was more talkative than her brother. When Alec carried the bread and tea out to the men, she told Ruth and Penny that she wanted to get away, far away from Ireland, to Australia or Canada. Then she mentioned the dance in a tired way as if she was too old to enjoy it herself but that Ruth, still a child, might have a good time.

"If you tell Alec which is your box, he'll probably bid high for it."

"Father's in the barn," Alec said to Katie when he returned. "He'll not be in for a while yet."

Ruth bit into the soft bread and let the taste of sweet homemade jam linger in her mouth. Alec's accent, the look of him, the sturdy lines of his body, the smell of hay on him, made her tongue-tied.

The eggs she and Penny took back to the cottage were large and brown with bits of straw sticking to them. They didn't smell of fish, and Aunt Hilda was actually going to use some of them for baking. At home, mother used powdered eggs for cakes. When she wanted one for breakfast she had to pick it out of the isinglass in the big jar in the cellar.

That evening, she and Penny cycled back to the farm. Alec was standing by the gate, waiting, and Katie came to join him. "We're going to look at Alec's wee house," she said.

They walked along the lane slowly, *Under the October twilight*, Alec and Ruth in front, Penny and Katie talking softly, following after. The small house stood in its own garden and Ruth knew that one day not too far off she would live here. It was a feeling as strong as any she'd ever had in her life. She knew it would be so as sure as she was standing there looking at the white-painted stone walls and the knotty brown door.

Alec opened the door and Ruth followed him inside.

"My uncle was killed. This was his place. He said I should have it."

"Killed in the war?" she asked.

Instead of answering, he showed her how his uncle had papered the wall round the grandfather clock and carefully avoided moving it.

"It's awkward, do you see. And there's the mechanism to consider."

"Will you move it?" she asked.

And he replied, "If you think it should be moved, Ruth. To decorate the walls."

She wanted to say to him, *A little house . . . A clock with weights and chains*, but his face looked closed to poetry. And there would be time. Years of time. Sitting by the little fireplace, the day's work done, she would read to him and tell him stories, like Scheherezade, to lift the heaviness of his moods.

She said to him, "If you move the clock, it might stop."

"Nothing will stop it," he answered. "There will always be someone to keep it going."

Next morning, cycling through Clanagh on her way to the farm, she saw Patrick Monaghan and tried to ride on quickly but he ran in front of her and got hold of the handlebars.

"Here I am, Ruth," he said. "It's Saturday and you're to come to my brother's house. We'll be having a grand party. I've told them of you, Ruth. That you're a fine, fine girl. And there's no need for them to know what you are. We'll get around that. I don't care that you're one of them. So meet me by the corner there. At eight o'clock. It'll be dark. You won't be seen."

"I can't," she answered. "I'm going to the dance with my cousin."

He stood there in his new suit. A 'utility' suit that would last but never look smart. Her father would have taken a bit of the material between his finger and thumb and pronounced it 'shoddy.' Patrick stayed quite still, letting go of her bike, waiting perhaps for a better answer. And it was then she'd had a chance to tell him she was only fifteen but all she could think of to say before she rode on was, "It was nice meeting you."

◆

Her dress, trimmed now at the neck, gave her, Penny said, an older look. Twenty at least. Her own black skirt and red blouse made Penny, Ruth thought, appear to be about thirty-five. They would put lipstick on outside so that Uncle couldn't see.

On the steps of the village hall, two guards in green uniforms were looking over everyone who entered. Inside, a fiddler and an accordionist were playing a kind of fast jerky music she found hard to follow. The dancers were crossing their feet and and stepping quickly, smiling at each other, clapping their hands.

When the music stopped, all the men went to one side of the room and the women gathered by the table with the boxes on it. The fiddler picked up the first box from the pile on the table and said, "What am I bid for this pretty thing?"

Ruth held her breath while boxes tied with fancy ribbons were auctioned off and men stepped forward to claim a partner. There were only three left when the fiddler held up hers. Alec paid half a crown for it and came to take her hand.

"I bought it for Hilda's cake," he said as they sat side by side, eating egg sandwiches. He told her he didn't dance well but when the music began again, he held out his arms to her like a prince in a story. It was the day before her sixteenth birthday and she had never felt so happy.

He was dancing with her and she saw herself in the cottage baking soda bread but employing someone else to do the rest of the work so that her arms wouldn't get red like Katie's. She was in his arms and in bed lying under a homemade quilt, sleepless, holding his hand. In two years, school over, she would return to marry him and all this would come true.

The music changed to another jig and she tried to learn the steps, crossing her feet one over the other, laughing at her own awkwardness. Alec, smiling at her, said, "You'll soon get the way of it."

He stopped smiling when a man she'd seen at the farm came to talk to him, keeping in step, all three of them dancing oddly together. Ruth followed their glance and saw two dark figures by the door, the guards trying to pull them back.

There was a rush of movement. She was dancing on her own. The music grew louder. Penny pulled her away from the jumping, stepping crowd. They were outside. They were beside Katie's old car and there he was, Alec, lying on the back seat, bleeding. She tried to get in beside him to wipe the blood off her new love's face but Penny pushed her into the front seat. Katie drove very fast, not to the farm but to a darkened house in a place whose name Ruth never learned.

The next Monday, Uncle Brian said, "You'll understand. They're not to be encouraged." He gave her a parcel of eggs and butter and told her that rationing would soon be over. When the train pulled away and she looked out to wave at him, she saw only his back.

In Bradford, on the station platform, her father was waiting. He put his arms round her but it was different, as if in those few days she had changed, had become a member of a secret society. She could smell the brilliantine on him and felt stupidly glad that he kept his black hair smoothed down. He kissed her and picked up her suitcase.

"I heard about young Alec," he said.

She made no connections for him and only asked how the boys were and if the weather had been good. School started again next day and she had work to finish.

Alexander. First childish love. They had stood here in this very room years ago, dreaming different dreams. And there he was at the door, holding out his hand to her.

"Alec," she cried out, "Alec!" as if life had reeled backwards and they were to be allowed another chance and would get it right this time.

But it was only the window cleaner wanting his money.

"The men were shot by their own side for unacceptable behaviour."

Ruth turned the radio off. All the angry sorrow of the place would drive her out soon, she knew. Meanwhile, she made her way to the clock, put her hand behind it, took the key from its hook, and opened the glass door in the front to wind it up. Alec had been right. It would never stop. There would always be somebody willing to keep it going.

PUB LUNCH

*"For there is no friend like a sister
In calm or stormy weather."*

—CHRISTINA ROSSETTI, *Goblin Market*

They were sitting at a small table by the fireplace waiting for bread and cheese and beer. And waiting to begin their conversation as if the food and drink would free their tongues for them, hers at least. Romaine's mouth was closed tight. Ellen tuned in to the voices of the customers nearby.

"He said he'd break every pot in the house if she went to Blackpool."

"What could I do? I took her umbrella."

"He wanted his ashes scattered up near Haworth."

Their remarks brought in the surrounding countryside, drew the moors nearer and reminded Ellen that there were villages and farms and bleak old dwellings and miles and miles and miles of dry stone wall going up hill and down which she had never seen and might not, now.

"That's what he said, scatter my ashes on Top Withens. He loved that place."

"He ran off shouting that sex made no difference."

"And this election. They're all rubbish. Don't vote.

That's what I say."

Once upon a time, sitting together like this, she and Romaine would have picked up a random phrase and made a story out of it, laughed about the ashes at Haworth, giggled at the man for whom sex made no difference, fought over the election. But that was years ago.

And those years were between them now like a metal shield. Ellen looked around for the waitress. Romaine took a slip of paper out of her purse and put it back again, snapping the gilt clasp shut. Outside in the town, the sun was shining on damp trees that were nearly leafless, people were crowding round the stalls in the street to buy fish and handkerchiefs and brass ornaments and sheepskin slippers.

Out there, Raffi Patel was shouting, "Come on, ladies. Everything half price. New stock comes next week. We need space in the van for it. Money to pay for it. Come along, ladies." And the ladies were stopping to pull aside a red skirt or a blue one and to feel the material with their sensitive fingers. One thing they knew was cloth, these Yorkshire women.

This wasn't Romaine's usual pub. But since their lunch in the Three Crowns five years ago, Romaine had not been back. At least not with Ellen. The Dog and Gun, scene of their 1989 quarrel, held no happy memories either. And the Shepherd's Crook, Romaine's true local, was, she said, being re-decorated, done into Sherwood Forest green and fake oak.

Leaving the house that morning, she had simply said, "The Cock and Bottle at 12. I expect you'll find plenty to amuse yourself till then."

Ellen had held herself back. She could not, on her first morning, open the front door and shout down the street at her retreating sister, *What do you mean, amuse! Do you think I've come here for amusement?* Instead she sat in the dining room eating toast and marmalade and staring at the photograph of herself and Romaine aged seven and ten. It was a posed portrait, she was sitting on a stool and Romaine, standing slightly behind her, rested one hand on her sibling's shoulder. Romaine's dark hair was streaked now with grey but the sharp blue eyes that looked out of the frame had lost nothing of their demanding expression. Ellen was a chubby blonde then, an amiable, persuadable younger child. Their shapes hadn't changed much. She had never reached Romaine's height and only kept her weight down by bouts of self-denial. She went to the kitchen and put another slice of chunky brown bread in the toaster.

The waitress had two thick white plates on her tray. Each one held a cottage loaf, a hunk of cheese, a tomato slice, lettuce, and a pickled onion.

"Who's the Stilton?"

"She is," they both replied.

"Your beer's at the bar," the waitress said, setting down knives and forks wrapped in paper napkins, talking to them sharply as if she knew enough not to like them, as if Romaine, being with a stranger, had herself become a foreigner overnight.

And yet this was Romaine's home. In her green tweed skirt and brown sweater and cord jacket, she looked like the other women at the tables round about. Her voice was similar to theirs. Her face had a look of being set against all invaders, ready as their forefathers had been to repel Vikings and Scots, tribes from the South, and anyone else who came to pillage and rob and deny.

"I ordered the Cheddar," she said.

"I did," Ellen replied, as Romaine reached over to change the plates. "I don't like Stilton."

"Don't like Stilton! You used to order it all the time. A Stilton ploughman's. I can hear you saying it over and over again. You do like it."

"I do not. I've never liked it since Dad told me it was full of microbes."

"You . . . " Romaine bit her lip.

Ellen let her sister change the plates and began silently to nibble at the white parts of the blueish cheese, hating it, watching for worms to crawl out of the tiny holes.

I have come here, she said to herself, as a one-woman ambassador of goodwill. Sisters should be friends. It is decreed. By whom? And when had there ever been peace between them? Christmas 1980: In the kitchen there was Romaine, her thin face relaxed and lovely, singing all the carols she knew as she pushed bread and sage into the turkey. Before they opened their gifts, she'd put her arms round Ellen and wished her a merry, merry Christmas. The fight had begun after dinner over the dishes. You took the Worcester plates to Toronto. You had no right. They're all I have. But briefly that day there had been goodwill in the old house.

Romaine went to the bar. She was decisive. The quick one, their mother always said. With a name like hers,

Romaine would reply, she had to be sharp. She never bothered to tell people that her parents had met in Paris and discovered they were both admirers of Romain Rolland. When the writer died in the year their daughter was born, they gave her his name to preserve their happy memory although the writer himself was beyond caring and no one in the family understood.

Ellen saw their mother and father clearly, meeting in a bookstore on the Boul' Mich, touching hands, reading much into the chance that had led them to that shelf at the same moment, under the r's. She saw them young and bright, him dark and tall and her with brown hair freshly curled that morning, an eager student. She watched as Romaine, slim and assured, shouldered her way through a group of customers, drawing back as beer was spilt on her hand but still smiling. She was among her own people. This was her nation, her country. And Ellen had a passport of another kind.

Perhaps they should have met in Paris this time and let that ancient love affair endow them with goodness. They might have met a man each under different letters, p or q, t or o. Both of them now were, after all, getting on for fifty. It was time to bury the old hatchets. Ellen was prepared to say, *Can't you forgive me, Romaine?* A life lived so far on the principle of accepting blame if offered, but never actually looking for it, was about to change. Going back in time to childhood, a school day, dropping out of the team, letting down ten other girls at once, Ellen had not apologised although guilt had been directed at her like a host of poison-tipped arrows.

And here she was now, prepared to say, *Can't you forgive me*, without being aware of her true crime.

On her last visit, her father had scarcely known who she was. *Well you've been away so long. I have another life, Dad.* But she had not said, *Sorry, Dad, I deserted you*, although Romaine had hovered over the mourning period waiting to hear her say those exact words.

In Toronto she'd built herself a fortress. High up from the ground she lived, protected from invasion by the doorman and a two-way phone. She'd put her life together with care. The windows were slits through which no enemy fire could penetrate. And the view over the city was whatever she chose to make of it. Her working life was below, among the scurrying, hurrying figures, among the tall buildings, in the sky itself. Her kind of life.

So·what had she hoped for, coming back for the seventh time in eleven years? Instant love? Desperate reconciliation? *You are my only living relative*, she wanted to shout at her sister. *Does that mean nothing? Was it all my fault? Always!*

She reached over quickly and cut a chunk off the cheddar on the other plate. Romaine put the two glasses of bitter on the table and pushed one towards Ellen. Then she saw the yellow rhombus lying there with the bread and lettuce and shrugged her shoulders.

"Well," she said, and again, "well?"

Ellen tore the top off the roll and put it into her mouth, conscious of its whiteness. It was still wheat, they said, still good, but to her it lacked virtue. When she had chewed it, she said, "I'm going to look round the church this afternoon. I haven't been there in years."

"It's your holiday."

"Yes, it is."

"You could've gone to France, to Italy, to America. Spending all this money."

"It's my money."

"Right," Romaine said, implying she'd had to come over here to throw it around, to feel superior.

She pushed the pickled onion off her plate with the fork. She had never liked pickled onions. Then she took a mouthful of beer and slowly swallowed it. She looked at Ellen as if she was approaching from a long way off. As if, in order to see her, she had to cast aside her working day, her office thoughts, her morning of memos and queries and face-to-face encounters with people whose supplementary benefits were about to be stopped.

Did Romaine spend her days saying to sad people, *We know you've been working, Mr. or Mrs. So-and-so. You've been seen. Reported. It's against the rules. Rules that are designed entirely for your benefit?*

Ellen shrank back in the face of her sister's supplicants. And yet in her own office over there in that palace of glass and consumer delight, she herself dealt out other cruelties. *I'm sorry we can't give you a loan, Mr Giancarlo. Another mortgage on your house is out of the question.*

"Things don't change much here."

"I would've come to meet you in Manchester, Ellen."

"It's a long drive."

"Would've saved you the train fare."

And the cost? Romaine didn't mention a price. And Ellen didn't explain that she wanted to make that part of the journey alone. She needed time to look out of the train window at the changing countryside, to watch out for the crooked spire and then the hills themselves and, as the train pushed on at great speed, to hear in her head the lines of Country songs: 'You picked a fine time to leave me, Lucille.' 'Thank God and Greyhound, she's gone.' 'Can't you forgive me, Romaine.'

But by the time she arrived at the station, another voice was saying aggressively, *What did I do to her? Why am I always in the wrong? What have I ever done to her?*

The plane had been late. She'd caught a later train and had forgotten that in this small town, taxis didn't hang around waiting to be hailed. It was dark when she finally arrived at the house. The meal was cleared away. Yet in Romaine's anxious face there was something of the past. But she had merely shown Ellen to her room and said she hoped it would be comfortable. Any Bed and Breakfast landlady would have said the same. So Ellen had lain there awake, sad, noticing relics from their old home which all remained here though some of them were small enough to be carried away. Even the patchwork quilt, nearly a hundred-years-old by now, could be rolled up and taken. But she had not come as a thief.

After two nights she would move on. There was London. There was Scotland. There were plenty of places for her to go where she could see sights and write postcards to her friends. *Wish you were here,* which translated into, *I am lonely. The scenery is not enough.*

She was now three thousand miles from Toronto and the kindness of her friends. The day before yesterday in the Cafe Espresso on Baldwin Street, Marie had poured cream into her coffee and said, "Don't set too much store by this trip, Ellen. Your life's here. This is where your home is. Where the people who love you are." And at the office, they'd said, "Have a pint of beer for us," all of them wishing her well but looking at her sadly as though every single one of them had made a journey like this and knew exactly how it would end.

Romaine said, "You do like it. You're eating it."

"Only the white parts."

Their parents, touching hands in that bookstore across the Channel, had put a burden on their first-born. Romaine would be an intellectual, would write great books too and one day they would return to Paris and see her name on those same bookstore shelves. Ellen was named for the great-aunt who had made the quilt. The first birthday gift she could remember was a kit for threading beads on string.

The Cock and Bottle had moved upmarket. The wallpaper was from Central Pub Decor; the beams were plastic, the fire burning in the old stone fireplace was fuelled by gas, the flames following the same pattern always. Only the customers had aged.

The barman came over and said, "Remember me, Ellen? Haven't seen you for years. Thought you'd got lost over there in that wild place. My Mum's sister went to live in Canada. A place called Thunder Bay. Is that near you?"

Ellen shook her head. She could have drawn a map for him, moved the beer mats about and outlined the shape of Canada in crumbs of cheese from sea to shining sea: British Columbia, Alberta, Saskatchewan all the way to the rocky coast of Newfoundland. "It's a big country," she said.

Romaine was tapping her foot on the floor and looking at her watch as if there was only now and not all the rest of time. But Ellen held on to the barman, a lifeline in a red shirt, and wanted to tell him that she had not meant to come back. She could have spent the money on a trip to Vegas with desert sun, bright lights, a chance of great wealth, and eaten breakfast every day with gamblers.

"Thunder Bay," she said, "is at the top of Lake Superior. It's a thousand miles from Toronto. Just inside the border."

He was edging away, not interested in a geography lesson. Years ago, she recalled, he had planned to own a pub himself and did not, yet. So he too hated her for having a life in another place and returning to see his failure.

"Two more halves of bitter, please," she called after him.

And then she picked up, through Romaine's silence, a few more words from strangers.

"He was playing away."

"What if I don't vote and every other bugger does?"

"So they put his ashes into three jars, urns like, and each of us got some."

"Did you hear what that woman said?" she whispered to Romaine. For a moment there was a flicker of old times in Romaine's eyes, a memory of those days when they were young together and had played this game over their first glasses of cider; listening, watching, commenting, making up lives for others long before they had invented lives for themselves.

"You've never understood," Romaine said, and let those few words stand for fifteen years of perceived neglect, of unanswered letters, a dying father, a lost cat. Her words were spoken with the broad vowels and solid consonants which she had held on to; she had not betrayed her past and her language like some others, one in particular sitting not three feet away.

And another thing, she might have said, *you have had more hours of sunshine than I will ever have. Look out there at the landscape I have had to put up with all this time.*

Ellen looked out of the window at the hills and remembered when they had ridden their bikes down the bumpy side of the moor, laughing and shrieking, taking a mad shortcut to the road by the reservoir, breaking ice on the March puddles.

She dragged another memory from some fold in her mind and offered it to her sister. "When we used to go to Hammonds for tea, wasn't there a man called Harry? A kind of clown who talked to the children, told us jokes?"

"James. His name was James. And he wasn't a clown. He was a head waiter. He wore a black suit and tie."

So James appeared again and they were little girls dressed in kilts and hand-knitted sweaters and Mother sat between them, smiling at them both, proud of them, of her handiwork. And James, a kindly hand on each small head, justified his salary by asking them if they were enjoying their cakes.

"I've always thought he was a clown."

"You would, wouldn't you. You see life as if it was a joke, a bloody circus."

"Maybe it wasn't Hammonds."

"Oh that's right. Change the place. Just so that you're right! You have to be right, always right. You do like Stilton."

People round about were looking at them, noting their phrases. *You do like Stilton!* They would take that one home and repeat it to their friends: Two middle-aged women, perfectly normal-looking, quarrelling about cheese.

"I have never liked Stilton."

And then Romaine began again as if the food and beer had indeed loosened her tongue. She took a deep breath and Ellen was reminded of a play she had seen about Sarah Bernhardt. Like an actress turning to face the audience, Romaine let the words flow from her in a rush of air.

"You think it's only about cheese, don't you? You come back here and I know that a whole fortnight of my life is going to be ruined. Every time I think this will be different, this time she won't start something, this time I won't be lying awake at nights going over what she's going to say, to deny."

"Me start something!"

"When father was sick, where were you?"

"I offered to come."

"Do you have to stay over there?"

"It's my home now."

"You've never once invited me."

"I have. And you were so . . . so righteous about it."

"Righteous!"

"You've always been righteous."

Ellen turned away, pulled her jacket closer round her shoulders and sat there as if she were quite alone.

Romaine went on, "When we were still at school and visitors came to the house . . . "

And Ellen listened because Romaine was now going back to their beginning.

". . . Dad would say, 'Ellen is my clever daughter.' And where was I in all that? You tell me. 'We named Romaine after a great writer but it's our Ellen who'll surprise us one of these fine days.' And what's been so goddam surprising about your life. You tell me that!"

You're my sister, Ellen wanted to shout out. But what she did actually say, softly, was, "What's surprising about my life is that I had the courage to leave this place. I got away. I left. I didn't stay here to be a martyr. I wanted a different life. I got it. Do you think it's been easy?"

The table tipped. Plates fell to the floor, crumbs of bread, chunks of cheese, bits of lettuce fell round her feet and onto her skirt. Romaine stood up and gathered her purse and umbrella.

Ellen watched her go, tall, thin, smartly dressed. Romaine, angry, implacable, all that was left of her family, her only close relative in the world. Sensible feet in good shoes were taking her down the street to the town hall, to her office inside it, behind an old wooden door which would soon close. Close tight.

Brushing lettuce off her lap, Ellen jumped up and ran, ran after her sister down the street and yelled so loudly that passers-by stopped and stared.

"All right. All right, then. I don't care. I won't ever

come back and ruin your days. Goodbye. And I do not like any kind of blue cheese."

Romaine turned sharply then, almost slipping on the damp pavement and came running back towards her along the cobbles, past this audience of people she knew, past stallholders and shoppers, her arms held out, her hair falling, late now for work.

And it took all of Ellen's courage to stand still there beside Raffi's stall, with Raffi shouting, "Come on ladies, everything's got to go," and wait for Romaine because she wasn't sure whether her sister was coming back to her for love or for revenge. Or how she would tell the difference.

THE VIEW FROM HERE

Six

"I don't much care where," said Alice.
"Then it doesn't matter which way you go,"
said the Cat.

—LEWIS CARROLL, *Alice in Wonderland*

It was a journey. It was a journey she'd planned in advance. The red line on the map showed the way, a long road across a paper landscape. As she travelled, she would tear up the scenery behind her, shred it, leave the scraps for birds to line their nests with.

She lined up in the dark shed with other dimly lit people and shuffled forwards when the driver opened the door of the bus.

"You going all the way?"

"More than likely."

"S'what your ticket says."

She looked at her watch when the bus set off.

"You're leaving early," she said but no one paid any attention.

As the bus turned left by the Thrift shop, she asked, "Is this the right way?"

The driver didn't hear, or pretended not to. If he wanted to make a mystery tour of the trip east along the Trans-Canada, let him. She only wondered about the people who turned up at the bus station and found their transport gone.

Lights in the houses were going out as they left the city behind. Lights of cars streamed by in the other direction and in the distance loomed the dim shapes of the Coastal Range. The other passengers were settling down for the long haul, for the next day and the night after that. There was already a smell of stored food and by the time they got to Calgary, the bus would reek of cold meat and oranges and cheese. Music was leaking from somebody's Walkman, an irritating undercurrent that could quickly drive a person berserk.

With all the thoughts that were going round in her head, sleep was a non-starter. Her life had become a maze of if-onlys. If only they hadn't found out. If only she could keep on working. If only it could be kept from his mother. If only she'd known what he was doing.

The bus came to a halt beside a strip mall that appeared to have been set down by aliens and abandoned, and the driver said, "Ten minutes here. Restroom at the back of the coffee shop. I do not wait."

She got out and left her backpack on the seat, window seat, third row in. She'd chosen the place especially, wanting to be near the front. For escape perhaps.

Sleepy figures lumbered into the convenience store and bought coffee in styrofoam cups, clumsily fitting the little lids on to prevent spillage. She bought a bottle of water because she wanted something she could see through.

"Does anyone come in here at night?" she asked the young woman behind the counter, curious to know if they kept the place unprofitably open for a few travellers.

"Maybe."

It was a different population. Day people had direct answers. Those who worked while others slept were cagy, seemingly reluctant to part with words or give opinions.

"I suppose," she answered, not wanting to offer more words than might be expected.

The bus took off again and before long the little garbage bag tacked to the wall beside her was full of her tears. She had used up all her Kleenex and now her tears would drip onto the floor and form a pool. Alice, Alice, Alice, she said to herself. But there was no lizard, no rabbit. She had to remain, for the moment, Emma. Emma who had decided three days ago that she must leave and had now, finally, left.

You've packed very little, an imaginary interviewer said, thrusting a microphone that looked like a furry animal's leg into her face.

Where I'm going, I won't need much.

To a monastery? A convent?

I'm going to ride to the edge and fall off.

Is this wise?

I am driven by desperation. The bus is driven by Roger Staines. It says so on a board above his head. Send complaints and praise to the bus company. Always mention his name.

"If you're too hot, too cold, tell me," Roger Staines said.

What if I'm too afraid, too out of synch with everybody

86

else? When your world falls in, what can you do but crawl out from under the wreckage and find a new one?

"Space! I want space," she recalled shouting. Shouting it into space because Donald for that moment was deaf. Donald was lying half under the piano, the dog panting anxiously round him. When she asked if it was true, he had only offered a sickly glance in his own defence.

How heavy is a last straw? How long is a piece of string? Answer in both cases the same: As heavy or as long as it needs to be.

Of course I am running away. From the office, the house, the street, the consequences.

I intend to keep running till the land runs out and there's a cliff, a certain end to things.

I'm going to a lemming convention.

Yes I could have flown but I need time. Is there a sense of greed in asking for both time AND space? Does it have to be either or?

You have been accused. What terrible words. And no one had said them aloud to Donald, yet. It was like looking into a deep pit and seeing a host of angry faces looking up.

"Hope!" Roger shouted, waking up the sleepers in his dormitory on wheels.

"What!" she called back. Who was he to be telling her what she should feel? What did he know? She'd told him nothing. There was no hope.

But that's where they were. The town called Hope, set in a valley where a lot of people lived—in hope.

"Well-known for its chainsaw carvings but hard to see them in the dark."

She watched the moon dancing in the trees ahead, leading them on like a jack-o'-lantern.

Two women and a boy got off at the next place, a gas station just off the highway. A car drew up and honked its horn. Roger waited and two teenagers with backpacks and bedrolls hopped out of the car, staggered across the lot and climbed on to the bus.

"Banff?"

"Tickets?"

"Yeah."

"I'll get them later."

The door closed and the bus moved onto the road again.

The teenagers disturbed the quiet that had arranged itself over the other passengers. A boy and a girl, they shuffled and giggled and one of them kicked an empty coke can out into the aisle. But gradually the night overcame them too.

She had, after all, slept. They were going by a long lake. It was early morning. Families in houseboats were getting up and having breakfast. Laughing at their own innocence. Looking forward.

And where were her fellow passengers going? All the way across the country, to Toronto and then further east to the other coast perhaps. For reasons of work or escape or love? She counted twenty, old and young, on a variety of journeys. Across the aisle a woman with grey curly hair had let her knitting fall to the floor. Emma leaned over and picked it up and put it back on the woman's lap. A square of white and pink. Its softness made her want to cry again.

The woman woke and said, "I have to finish this by Winnipeg," and began to coil the wool over the needles as if she'd never stopped.

Well Donald, when the truth is out, what then? The information highway is full of potholes. This you should've known. And who was she anyway? You're supposed to be smart. And you let someone in on the company's secrets. It's not the end of the world, you said. But it is. You have gone beyond.

Roger Staines pulled the bus over to the side of a road on the edge of nowhere. A youngish man climbed on. Long wavy hair, leather jacket, broad shoulders. A biker who had lost his bike? A man who rode about the country terrorising people with his speed and sound? His face looked set against the world. He sat down in the seat everybody else had avoided, directly behind the driver.

He was a pirate, a raging maniac who would stick a gun in Roger's back and say, *Drive us to New York.* He would hold up gas stations en route and shout, *fill-er-up*, and never allow the passengers to get off and the washroom at the back of the bus would become a stinking pit. They would come to blows over fragments of food.

Donald I am in New York living with a long-haired man. I am into leather.

Or maybe he was into short term crime and this was how it ended. He was in it with Roger. Cash. Jewels. Rape. Emma whimpered. Roger turned and said,

"You cold? You should've said."

Kindness to lull her into feeling that he was her friend? Or would the biker turn and demand that passengers hand over their money and jewels? She glanced round. Not many Rolexes here. Like her, the other passengers were wearing jeans and sweaters, comfortable clothes. Not one of them looked like a silicon millionaire.

She moved to the window and hugged her backpack closer.

When they stopped for breakfast a woman got on, thirtyish. She greeted Roger and the biker as if they were old friends. She heaved a bag on to the rack and sat in the seat by the door. Neatly dressed, probably not in collusion with the biker. Though clever crooks never made things obvious. How many kilometres before the other two drew her into their conspiracy?

Emma bought coffee, looked at the buns in the glass case on the store counter and felt as though she would never be hungry again. A few passengers stood smoking by the side of the road. The others stayed on the bus and ate the fruit and muffins they'd brought with them.

Everybody on? They set out again towards the Rockies.

"Why did you set off early? In the schedule it says half past midnight."

She had to ask. She had to ask because it would have been foolish not to. And by now some of her certainties had been left behind.

Roger took a hand off the wheel and pointed to a sign that read, "Do not engage the driver in conversation."

He was a big man, greying hair. His jacket hung on the hook provided.

She woke from a dream of a dancing piano, and heard the soft murmur of voices. They were plotting. The biker, the driver and the thirtyish woman. Emma pushed back the hardness of the past few days and listened for hints of criminal intent.

Roger said "So how're the kids, Jean?"

"You'll talk to her and not me," Emma said, but it was as if she spoke to the air.

The young woman sighed. "I'm doing my best but you know how it is. S'hard these days with kids. Got to know where they're at. Me away three days a week."

"I know what you mean," Roger said, not turning.

"You got to make sure they have a sense of responsibility early on. And loyalty." That was the 'biker' speaking.

Loyalty to what? To whom? Emma wanted to shout.

To Donald? To his mother? To myself? To the company? Tell me!

"I don't think," Donald had said, two days ago, "that there is any need to discuss this with Mom."

Because his mother was lying in a hospital bed attached to an intravenous drip. He was right. This was no time to tell her that she should have taught her son more about responsibility. Explanations to his mother-call-me-Penny ran and re-ran in Emma's head. He was not a scapegoat. Not just a scapegoat. He should have known.

The non-stop click of knitting needles was pricking words into her brain.

Jean was saying, "There's so much trouble. A lot of bad kids. Some days you just want to keep them out of jail."

"Like my kid brother," the 'biker' said. "Stupid. Been to see him. No sense. It's killing my Mom."

"I'm sorry," Roger said. "What'd they give him."

"Six months. He's scared out of his mind. Scared out of his stupid idiot mind."

There was silence for a while as the inside of a jail cell enclosed them all.

"There's a lack of example higher up," Roger stated.

"What it is," the 'biker' said, "is the politicians don't make it easy. What are they thinking of besides the next vote? You don't like to think they're all crooks and fools but they kind of give that impression."

Jean said, "My Dad's been after them about his pension for years. Got a file this thick. And still they want him to pay taxes."

"Taxes! I've got this plan but there's no way they'll go for it. You just have to take from everybody a simple percentage of what they earn. No need for all this form-filling. A simple, straight percentage. I worked it out while I'm driving."

"They don't, if you notice, go for anything simple," the 'biker' said and sighed.

Jean leaned over to Roger and asked, "She any better?"

"Not a lot. She's in for more treatment. The doctors don't tell you much."

In that moment, Emma, if she'd had one, would've handed over her Rolex without a word. The bus was filled with trouble. The accumulation of sorrow pressed on her chest like an airbag.

Last evening, Donald, hearing her speak, had lifted his head, banged it on the underside of the baby grand and lain back down again. And she had yelled at him that it was no use getting drunk. No help in that at all.

He'd murmured, she thought. She thought she'd heard the words "Don't go."

By now he must have known she was gone. He would've come to, shouted her name, looked out to see the car still there and searched for a note. He was making coffee and toast, calling her friends.

"The whole country seems to be just slipping south, if you ask me," the 'biker' said. "Jobs, doctors. Whatever."

"I get sick over the trees they're cutting. I drive east, I see all the bare mountains."

Jean said, "I've got a thirteen-year-old. A twelve-year old. If you don't teach them values."

Roger said, "A conscience. Important they have a conscience."

"But it's like the state of the world. The mess it's in. It makes you wonder. People killing people wherever you look. "

Roger said, "Responsibility. That's what it's about. Like me driving this bus. Being on time. Driving safe. Getting everybody on and off—with the right bags."

Jean said, "Only place I could find a job. Revelstoke. My Mom looks after them three days a week."

"No. Well. I mean you have to take what there is, right?" the young man who no longer looked like a biker said. Then he turned to Emma, "Sorry if you've been trying to sleep."

"I've been listening." *Listen to me you guys, the world isn't being fair to you. You have to scream out and yell and take better advice, get a second opinion.*

Before Emma could summon up the courage to tell them these things out loud, Roger said, "This is where she gets off."

Emma looked at the shelter by the side of the road and the coffee shop with its sign hanging down. This was her destination? She hadn't planned for this, only to keep going and going till she was out of reach. But obediently she stood up and took her pack down from the rack. She tried to gather words to tell the three of them to fight back, and began to say, "Could I . . ."

Jean ignored her and said to Roger and the 'biker,' "You know, I heard that when you look at it from outer space, earth is the most beautiful planet, green and blue, just awesome."

And the 'biker' replied, "Yeah," in a wondering tone, as if it he'd seen it for himself.

Emma stepped down.

Before he closed the door, Roger called out to her, "The bus you want'll be along soon."

Standing on the scrubby brown grass, Emma waved to her fellow passengers and silently wished them well: Jean's kids. The young man's brother. Roger's sick wife or mother or sister.

She watched the bus till it was out of sight. Did Roger Staines mean that she should turn round and go back home? What did he know? And what right did he have to tell her what to do?

The schedule on the wall told her that the times had changed and that there would be a bus back to Vancouver in three hours. Another, slower, bus to Calgary would come by in an hour. That was the bus she had meant to get. She had a choice. She could wait here and continue her journey east or cross the road and return to Donald, to Donald's mother, to all the attendant problems.

She went into the cafe and asked the waitress for two scrambled eggs with hash browns and toast, and ate them slowly.

Did Donald when he finally came to, sit up and bang his head on the underside of the piano again and was he lying there now unconscious? Did she care? Did any of it, cosmically speaking, matter? She had been set down by the side of the road and given time to ponder this.

She bought another bottle of water in the cafe, and a picture postcard of the mountains. She sat by the side of the road to wait and while she waited, she addressed the postcard to Donald and wrote, "I've found space and the view from here is awesome."

THE COLOUR OF SPACE

In daytime, the picture on the wall was of pink flowers on tall grey stems. In the dim dawn light it showed a man talking to a woman, looking up at her, his hand raised, pleading. Behind him a shadowy figure dissolved into a vase.

Emma got out of bed and walked to the window. Below, in snow lit by the parking-lot lamp, someone had walked carefully to tread out in large letters, DARCY WUS NOT HEAR. She was tempted to put her boots on and go down and stamp out, I WUS NOT LOOKING FOR HIM, but instead she crawled back into bed.

It was an hour before the sun would come up from over there towards Toronto and two hours before she was expected at Maid Mario. She stretched out in the double bed, star-like, reaching her feet and hands to the corners. She had left home in order to find space. And space there was, more space than she could handle; prairie stretching out beyond imagination and sky without limits. She had found space.

The elevator had already begun to clatter its way up

and down the shaft, taking the early workers to the street and bringing back office cleaners, transport workers, nurses; the men and women who owned the city by night. She envied them their power, their disdain for daylight, the empty streets. By the time she got down to Fifth Avenue, it would be crowded with people rushing to work, heads down against the snow and wind.

Mario was asking her to work overtime. She was in demand, he said. Every house she went to, they wanted her back. It's only because I'm cheerful, she told him. But in fact it was because she sat and listened to the clients, let them talk about their ailments. She dispensed a little advice and a suggestion here and there of a way to relieve their pains. She hadn't told Mario of her qualifications because she wanted to be accepted simply as out-of-work Emma who had travelled from Vancouver by bus in search of a job.

Occasionally in the past eight weeks she had considered returning home. She'd even thought of going to the bus station and waiting for Roger Staines. Perhaps on the return journey, he would talk to her about his life and ideas. But when she looked west, the mountains loomed like an insurmountable barrier, a wall of rock and snow-filled passes. The longer she stayed away, the higher the mountains became.

She had let Donald know where she was. She didn't want to be on any missing persons list. Now he called every weekend and pleaded with her to come back to him. All was well, he said. His mother was out of the hospital. The dog was pregnant. He was working things out with the company and his job would, probably, be safe although promotion from now on might be slow. Did she have to go off like that? It was only one night. He could have died lying there under the piano. And, by the way, the piano was gone. His brother had returned from India and sent movers to collect it.

He was sorry, very, very sorry. He would make it up to her. And besides, what about her job? She waited for him to say, *And what about your salary which pays half the mortgage?* But he hadn't mentioned money.

This early hour was made for contemplation. There was so much light from the street lamps that darkness was never total. There was always a glow in the small room. She lay there and considered her former life and the way she had left it, abandoned it, with only enough clean underwear for three days, her address book, and a pleasant feeling of irresponsibility. Which was followed by guilt. The guilt came on her in doses administered like the pain machine which gave patients the right amount of morphine on demand. As did the ultimate question: Why am I here?

Previous life: Early childhood, reasonable. College, a struggle between fun and work and anguish. Part-time jobs to make ends meet. Early death of father, piercing. Encounter with Donald seven years ago, romantic. Mother's domination of wedding plans, traumatic. Two incomes, no children. Capital accruing as he moved up the ladder in the new company. Future, bright.

"I am lucky," he'd said more than once, "to be in on the ground floor of this." The newness of the business excited him, brought a flush to his cheeks and made him want steak for dinner. They had invested in a three-bedroom townhouse and revelled in the space. Space which had been partly filled by the piano. Of course we'll take care of it, Donald had said without considering its size.

And now here she was like a bee in a hive living in a room twelve by twelve surrounded by others in similar cells, inhaling the cheesy smell of last night's microwaved lasagna. She got up, walked to the tiny kitchen area and plugged in the kettle.

Tending to the sick and the frightened day after day in the hospital in Vancouver had left her occasionally with the feeling that to be sick and afraid was normal. I don't know how you can be cheerful round those people, Donald's mother had said more than once, but that was before she herself had been laid low with a pulmonary embolism and needed nursing care.

"Why do you have to work Saturdays?" Donald had asked and blamed her for his fall. Oh he had repented. He was truly a faithful and caring man. But his one office fling with a petite blonde free of the smell of disinfectant who had wheedled secrets out of him and passed them on to a rival company, had brought him down.

Emma showered and pulled on the green polyester uniform, its pocket embroidered with Mario's whimsical logo of a pretty woman on a broomstick, over her tracksuit. The store-bought muffin, too sweet and too fatty, made her wish for her own kitchen. She threw half of it away, drank up her coffee, and made her way down to the hectic street.

◆

After five hours at the Harkman's, tidying the kids' rooms, cleaning the floors, doing the laundry, talking to the grandmother who was stiffened with arthritis, she went to meet Lisa at the Spur and Saddle.

Lisa had got there first and had ordered a couple of beers. They checked out the men in the room one by one and found them wanting. Too much muscle, that one. Narrow face next to him, a loser. Dark-haired fellow looking their way, sinister.

Against a few lovin' and leavin' songs from the cowboy on the small stage, Emma continued her story.

"I had to leave him, you understand."

"Did your parents die young?" Lisa asked.

"What do you mean?"

"You sound like a victim of early responsibility."

"Let's have another beer."

Mario had asked her to go to Mr. Berger's on Sunday but for once Emma said no; she liked the old man but she had plans. Her plans were to walk by the Bow River, stop for coffee in Kensington and then maybe go up the Tower and stare at the Rockies and consider her single future which stretched out like the prairies in the other direction.

She liked Mr. Berger. After he'd told her of the latest twinges in his hip joint, he showed her pictures of himself in the army in Holland. After the D-Day landing, he and his group had driven, walked, pushed, fought their way through Northern France and Belgium to liberate that flat landscape and its people. *They loved us there.* He didn't look much of a hero now, the old guy, but he had been a hero, and he knew it. One photograph in particular showed him, triumphant but exhausted, leaning against his army truck, a pretty girl on either side of him. Rotterdam, 1944.

It was unreasonable to expect men always to be heroes, especially when there were no wars to fight. But what Emma understood about old Mr. Berger was that his life had been perfect. He was a genuine hero and all round good man. She wished she could slip back in time to meet him, to be the one to welcome him home from war as he walked proud and straight, his brass buttons gleaming, along the station platform. He would have been faithful and true, their lives together a model of loving devotion.

"I can go back to Donald," she said to Lisa, "and try not to say 'You were lucky to get away with it,' or I can go on living here, get back to hospital work and start over."

Lisa replied that she was tired of hearing about Donald and his problems and that it wasn't hard to meet men if you went to the right places, but in her view Donald was just a guy who had lost his way for a moment. Possibly what he needed was trust and love. And anyway what if someone had moved in with him. "I mean, wouldn't that bother you?"

Emma pondered this and sorted through a list of women he would be likely to invite to take her place. Short and blonde? Tall and dominating? Soft and cuddly? Could he, Donald, possibly attract someone ravishing?

"You have to get used to the idea, there are no perfect men," Lisa said.

"There used to be," Emma replied, thinking of Mr. Berger. "There were once."

"In life they start out perfect and turn rotten. In stories, they start out rotten and then are discovered to be perfect." That was Lisa's statement. Lisa was living with a disc jockey whom she rarely saw. He worked till four in the morning and slept till noon. Her cleaning schedule kept her out all day and she returned to their apartment whacked out. It was, she said, ideal.

Emma found herself sitting with Mr. Berger on Sunday morning after all. The Rockies would always be there. The arc of blue sky against the white of the snow made the world too big for her to cope with. She wanted a smaller space, confined, framed, and a story she already knew.

While she was in the kitchen making coffee, he called out, "Seventy-three times twelve divided by three?" He did sums in his head to keep his mind sharp. She put the milk back in the fridge and multiplied seventy-three by four and called back, "Two hundred and ninety-two."

He seemed smaller than the week before and had only managed to get one sleeve of his tweed jacket on. She offered to help him but he said he liked it that way with one arm free. It reminded him of Italy.

"Were you there in the war?"

"I'm talking about after. Long after. Dolly had always wanted to go to Rome but nothing prepared us for

Rome in 1969. You couldn't imagine. Dolly—well. It was inside the church. You see, she was overwhelmed by the grandeur of it and the colour and the . . . "

He often stopped mid-sentence as if his mind had wandered to another place that was more interesting. At other times words poured out of him like water from a broken main.

Emma imagined the pair of them, Mr. Berger and Mrs. Berger, middle-aged and amazed, standing in the Colosseum or in Santa Maria Maggiore, lost to history.

"Dolly and the Virgin Mary. It was like an infection, if you know what I mean. Quietness overcame her. Like a pale blue gown, I thought afterwards. I had lots of time to think—afterwards."

"Your wife left you? She stayed on in Italy?"

"My wife was here! At home."

He had become confused.

He reached for the photo album and riffled through the pages.

"There," he said. "There!" He pushed the book under her nose. "That's my wife. Bernice."

It was a picture of a woman in long skirt and lacy blouse holding a reluctant cat. Bernice looked at the camera with a smile, a smile of possession. She looked like a happy woman, a woman who knew about the comforts of life and a settled place.

Had Bernice died young?

"Dolly was my Dutch friend. I used to go over on business every year and spend two weeks with her." He flicked the pages of the album back to the army days, the Liberation. The heroes welcome. He pointed to the girl on his left. "That one. That's Dolly! She'd leave her husband for that time and meet me. Usually we went to France. Italy was a mistake. I hadn't reckoned on the colours, you see. The vividness. Idols everywhere. Dolly was overwhelmed."

Emma tried not to seem curious. She patted the cushions and straightened out the tablecloth and asked the old hero if he'd like her to do any laundry. He sank back into his memories, leaving her stranded. His face still held traces of the handsome soldier. His eyes didn't reflect an acceptance of age. And his mouth, for all the lines around it, held the promise of kindness, even of sensual enjoyment.

She went into the kitchen and tried to trace the source of the sour smell. Under the sink she found a carton with half an inch of stale milk in it. She put it by the door with the rest of the garbage to take out when she left.

"Dolly," Mr. Berger murmured softly, "was wearing blue herself, but it was dark blue, not virgin blue, and she came after all from a country where the religion is plain."

Emma brought him a cup of tea and a slice of the gingerbread he liked.

"She went home and told him everything, her dull stick of a husband. We'd had sex, we'd had fun, we had a kind of understanding. We knew each other. It truly was the colours that spoilt it, the grandness of that church with its high painted ceiling, its statues, its powerful scent. She became penitential, you see."

The old man was silent for a moment. He bit into the gingerbread and let the crumbs roll down his shirt.

"Twenty-five times two weeks. Nearly a year of our lives, gone."

"But you had the memories."

"Memories!" he snapped and a mouthful of crumbs flew into the air. "We could have kept on."

Mario's real name was Geoff and his wife loved him but didn't understand him. He'd come to pick Emma up in the company van. He thought it was time he got to know her better and offered to take her out to a Japanese place for sushi.

Squatting on the floor beside a table laden with small bites of food, worrying about raw fish, Emma told Mario that she'd been called back to Vancouver. Family problems. He was sorry. She was good. Her clients would be disappointed. He'd foreseen, somewhere in the future, a partnership, a business partnership, because she was smart and personable.

He wanted to take her to a motel but didn't press the matter when she said, "I'm not into that." He only looked at her as if he was wondering how she could pass up such a chance, and said, "I can see you're troubled. I just thought a bit of relaxing sex might help."

On her way out, Emma hadn't been able to resist asking Mr. Berger what Bernice had felt about Dolly and his expeditions, his little holidays.

"She never knew," he replied, with a certainty that left no room for questions.

Emma had waited to laugh till she'd closed his door. The ignorance of men was sometimes astounding. So, comfortable Bernice had kept silent and forgiven Mr. Berger and lived out the time with him; possibly she had even sympathised with him when he returned that year from Italy in distress. Perhaps he had brought her souvenirs which she pretended to like and put away at the back of the closet.

Before she went to her room to pack, Emma walked to the back of the apartment building and trod out in the softening snow, U DONT EXIST DARCY. It took her several minutes.

Seven

ABSENCE

How long ago Hector took off his plume,
Not wanting that his little son should cry,
Then kissed his sad Andromache goodbye –
And now we three in Euston waiting-room.

—FRANCES CORNFORD, 1948

1976

She saw him coming. There were a few moments of not quite knowing. And then the shape, the walk, the turn of the head, identified him. There was a carelessness in the way he walked, as if he didn't ever expect to be run down by a truck or attacked from behind by a large dog. Even now.

She turned to go into the house. The geraniums in the tubs either side of the door needed water but could wait. She wanted a few minutes to compose the right sentence, conjure up the right tone, the tone in which she might speak of lying down with him in rose petals as if they ever had.

The sharp smell of the bunch of mint in her hand reminded her that there were people in the house, friends expecting a slice off the fatted calf which was in fact a leg of lamb. She hid in the kitchen, wishing them all elsewhere. No welcome committee required. *You've always been too self-sufficient.* Mother's voice in her head. Put a good face on it then.

I will say to him, It's so good to have you home again. I will ask if it's really him. Have you changed? Do you remember? Or maybe I should recite a few lines of poetry. More likely I should sit and listen because he will have so much to tell. Or has he told it to so many strangers that the narrative thread has worn thin.

Or there could be silence while, at arm's length, they simply stared at one another. For days.

Her messages to him had been public and one way only. A fuzzy picture of him had appeared on TV. *We are safe and well-treated.* The forced smile of the captive hiding who knew what mental and physical injuries. *Your husband is a hero. Glorious. Miles Gloriosus.*

Two weeks since he was set free and yet he had not come back to her.

She took two cups from the shelf and then put them back and hunted around for two glasses that matched.

She could hear his voice. He was out there talking to Jack next door, telling him, no doubt, the story which had made him a celebrity. The story would cling to him like another skin and he, and she, would never be free of it.

You have been absent from me in the Spring and Summer and Fall and Winter and Spring again.

Would he want beer? Wine? He had been deprived. It would be like him to check out the grass first before he came inside to embrace her.

He had been far, far away. Out of life. Lost. Loveless. Unless? After a time, they do come to occasionally 'co-operate' with their captors, the official said. Some do. Not all. He was a faithful man. That she knew.

If he'd brought her a gift, it would most likely be something she didn't want.

"Honey," he'd said last time, bringing her a jar of cornflower nectar in a bee-hived shaped jar. That was after the row about the yard, three weeks before his trip to the Middle East. Eighteen months ago.

Choose the words carefully. Words that would mean something, persuade him to stay now. Gentle, loving words.

We might go for a vacation.

I have travelled enough.

I have been here, waiting. My mother was a woman who also knew how to wait.

Would he understand that she could have been forgiven for taking a lover?

Was it someone I know?

Does it matter?

It matters.

Two weeks ago he should have walked up the path as he was now doing. Three days ago he had been released for the second time. Always afraid of his pleasures, his joys, preferring them deferred, he had stopped en route to ask questions, claiming a slow drift back into his natural world. He had likely been asking strangers in bars, *What has happened in the world? I have been absent.* Others had taken his life and then when he stepped off the plane there had been one embrace only before hard-faced officials had taken him off for 'de-briefing.'

Weeks of longing, moments of hatred, hours of worry.

The fact that he was on the wrong side of every argument was more to be pitied than condemned.

And there is this, she would say, kissing him whether he had shaved or not.

For a moment, it didn't matter whether it was truly him or not. Any man would do.

She hated just then the men and women who had gathered there to help her through the difficult time. Friends and neighbours, they had taken to coming by every weekend, talking over each new development as if he belonged to them. Discussing the awful possibilities in low voices whenever she left the room. They had come to her and offered her their time. They'd been willing to let her cook for them, rarely bringing more than a bottle of wine to contribute to the feast. She had made stews and roasted turkeys and assembled acres of salad as they sat around the house feeling good because they were 'keeping her company.' Some of the men had offered to go to bed with her as if that would also be a favour.

You must be lonely.

I'm not that lonely.

Life must go on.

You must be prepared for the worst.

This is the worst.

And the story grew longer by the day and shorter every evening as she discarded page after page of pretence. It all boiled down to a few lines of truth or near truth.

He has been in danger.

Living possibly on cockroaches.

Using up his resources.

Is he the same man?

Travelling alters a person. He had chosen to go.

When they called, he went. She wasn't sure she could forgive him for that. Or for falling so easily into a trap.

When he came inside, the visitors would take him over.

There you are.

Tell us everything.

Good to see you back.

We have to drink to this.

But they had seen his face. They feared violent expulsion. She could hear them driving away. Wheels over gravel, in haste as if he had some murderous intent or carried with him the grime of his cave, or a foreign virus. They called to him as they retreated,

"Wonderful."

"Welcome home."

"See you soon."

A flash of light. A captured image. Head down he talks to one of the drivers, saying what? *Don't go. Do stay!*

But they are all going.

There was a feast for his return. Lamb roasting. Peas. Potatoes cooked with mint.

And he was at the door, standing with his hands either side of the posts, hesitating, not sure. If she said nothing, he might turn and go back the way he had come. He hadn't shaved off his prison beard, his eyes were bleak.

She stared back at him, the wanderer returned, and all the loving words fled from her mind along with the image of rose petals.

She reached out her arms and yelled, "Where the fuck've you been?"

1946

The place smelled of coal dust. The benches were grimy. A few children were standing around, quiet, not expecting gifts. The murmur of women's voices rose and lowered. Heads were turned towards the large gaping hole of the tunnel. It was a hot day and she had chosen to wear the blue flowered dress.

The wait would not have seemed so long if she hadn't arrived an hour early. "Go on with you," his mother had said. "I'll stay here with Penny." She was cooking a whole side of lamb, his mother was, a Canterbury lamb killed specially and shared with the neighbours.

She stood there apart from the others, not wanting to talk, not sure if she wanted the train ever to arrive.

But the train, relentlessly, was arriving, chug-chugging its way through the tunnel. Bringing men back from the other side of the world where summer was winter and spring was autumn and the fields were full of blood.

The women on the platform moved forward like the ripple of a rug shaken to get the dust off. A few yards from the edge they all stopped as if the same thought had hit them simultaneously. *Will I recognise him?*

They took a few steps back towards the wall as they were struck by a second and worse thought, *Will he know me?*

The train came alongside the platform. Doors banged open with a noise like a thousand doors. Men stepped down like a thousand men. Men moved towards women moved towards men. A fearful rush of love filled the hollow space. Cries and laughs echoed round them like a flock of cockatoos.

She knew he wasn't there. She would be the only one who had to turn round and go home by herself weeping because she had been deceived. She would have to tell little Penny that the father she had been expecting was a figment of her imagination, the drawings she had sent him were floating in the sea between here and Europe.

He had met another woman and had now four or five little children who spoke a foreign language! That thought brought a strange feeling of relief. She suppressed it and clung to the despair which was only proper in the circumstances.

All around her, men and women clasped together were leaving the station, two-headed beings, four-legged, newly-formed, their footsteps beat out the rhythm of retreat.

And then she saw him. Last out, last carriage, very end of the platform. He must know it was her, the only one left to be claimed like a wallflower at a dance. They walked slowly towards each other. An hour went by. A day. A year. The platform was ten miles long. They were approaching and getting further away.

It came to her and she wished it hadn't, that she might have gone off with any of the other men, these equally well-known strangers. She made her legs move one after the other, taking short steps.

There was a moment when she might easily have turned and fled.

They were close enough to touch. She could smell the rough cloth of his uniform. He reached out, her arm came up of its own accord and their hands met.

He hugged her close and when she wept, he would believe it was because he had returned and would be home forever now.

2000

For two years he had only seen her through a grille.

And before that rarely, and through a haze. It was too long a sentence for fifty grams but they said there was a record of possession, of being involved with dealers, of truculence. *She was born of my return, conceived in a dark space alone, her mother was in her late thirties.* He had stood up in the courtroom to shout at her accusers, "She had no chance." They'd made him sit down. They didn't know him. His celebrity had been short-lived. Photographs taken in a cave don't come out clearly.

Jail can do two things, the counsellor had said to him, as if he knew nothing of incarceration. It can brutalize or it can spiritualize. You must be prepared for either.

There are other options, he might have replied but didn't.

He prepared the house with care and baked two loaves of bread which he'd learned to do after Penny left. He loved the historical nature of his sourdough starter, handed on from one person to another, given to him by a woman he'd met in San Francisco two years before. Lying in its plastic bag like some sleeping life-form, it was willing to leaven the mix of flour and water and sugar whenever it was awoken.

His sister called again to say he was stupid and could expect no more help from her.

"There is a time," Nora said, "when doors should be closed." She didn't add, even on your own flesh and blood but she meant it.

Will my daughter return to what she was? he had asked the counsellor, the walls, the mirror, himself. None of them had given him a decent answer.

Don't come here, Dad, she had said. Please. Wait for me there. At your place.

The past eight years wove through his mind like the tape in his recorder. Hope and desperation made a pattern of low-coloured threads. Penny's half-closed eyes staring at him. The bleak For Sale sign, something so small, a square of wood nailed to a post, had given out the message: This marriage is over this house is empty there is no love here.

Nora called again and said, "Remember. It wasn't just possession. She was selling it."

"We are all desperate," he answered. "I have to see to my bread."

On his last visit, his child had asked, "Why do you keep coming?"

Her face had narrowed but her eyes were her mother's sad eyes. He had let them both down by standing in harm's way once too often. There was some small chance for redemption here, now. And he was taking it.

◆

Good behaviour brings its own reward. Words in cross-stitch on the sampler Penny had brought with her from her home in New Zealand.

No one ever smiled. There were no jokes, no moments of leavening in jailhouse conversations.

"If I'm not responsible, who is?" he had demanded of Nora.

"She is twenty-four," Nora had replied.

Conceived almost as soon as I got back from there in a room that smelled of roast lamb and mint.

He went to the little room he'd cleared out for her; it was clean, tidy, spare. And then he went to the car and got out the bag full of bears. There were twelve of them. White ones, brown ones, one in a yellow fisherman's hat, one the size of a small child, another that fit on the palm of his hand. In the store he had stood for five minutes in front of the koala bear as if it might speak to him in Penny's voice with the accent of its country. The assistant had broken the spell with a sharp, "That one too?" as if he was a pervert with a stuffed toy fetish.

He arranged them on the quilt in a row, not sure why. Something he should have done a long time ago? Something he wished someone had done for him? Their little glass eyes stared at him without approval.

There was a knock at the door, a gentle tap-tap. She was early. The bed was made. The house tidy. Flowers in the only container he could find, a jar that had once held pickled cucumbers.

He was ready with her name on his lips. *Catherine. Catherine. It will be all right now, sweetheart. Daddy is here.*

He opened the door and there was Penny holding an overnight bag. Disappointment and delight fed into his mind in two confusing streams. He wanted to be alone with Catherine. He wanted Penny to be his wife again. He did not want her to take any credit for the flowers, the food, the bears. He also did not want to share his guilt. He did not want her to leave. He wished she hadn't come.

"I thought," she said looking round at the flowers, the table set for two, the two loaves cooling on the counter, "that I should be here."

"Are you stopping?"

"But now I see there's no need."

He put his arms round her and hugged her close to him. She let her bag slip to the step.

Over her shoulder he saw Catherine coming towards them. She came close and then looked beyond them at the flowers, the table set for two, and began to walk away. He pushed Penny aside and shouted "It's for you. It's all for you."

"Catch her," he said and went back into the house, up the stairs two at a time. He gathered a number of bears in his arms and began to throw them out of the window one after the other. "See. These are for you, Catherine."

The bear in the yellow hat hit his daughter on the head. She stopped and sat down on the path. Penny was there. He ran down the steps and was beside them. They were all crying, reaching for one another's hands.

THE LAST WE HEARD

OF LEONARD

Eight

The last we'd heard of Leonard he was in Chicago working for an advertising agency. One of their clients was a well-known automobile distributor and another was a cut-price grocery chain. So much for true art. Metal and rubber and baked goods had become his muse. We rubber-stamped his file. Gone. One friend. Not dead but to be forgotten. As if we could!

We were in the singles bar at Yonge two blocks up from Eglinton. The barman had just asked, "Whatever happened to the long-haired guy, artist, used to come in here? Friend of yours."

"I don't know," I told him, and paid for the beer and rye and carried it back to the table.

"He was asking about Leonard."

"It wasn't our fault," Jenny said, taking her beer from the tray and swallowing two mouthfuls before she set the mug down.

"He'll be happier there," Fran stated, as if he was a pet we'd managed to place in a good home.

"Poor Leonard," murmured Alice.

I said, "It was his choice."

That was what my mother had said to me when I left Welland to come to Toronto. *It is your choice, Janice.* The words were printed on my soul. They carried with them an image of peaches in bushel baskets and stacks of plums surrounded by fruit flies, and the sour smell of Dad's wine-making seeping up from the basement.

We set Leonard aside for a moment to talk about dinner. Jenny said she didn't want anything much, she'd been out to lunch with Grant again. Fran had leftover quiche from Gourmet Delight in her bag. Alice had driven from Guelph and was too tired to care about anything but another rye. After the company had promoted her and moved her to the new store, our home-cooked meals had taken a definite downturn. So dinner became a non-event.

Alice took a long drag on her last cigarette of the day—Jenny's apartment was a smoke-free zone. Fran pushed her way to the bar to get pretzels and chips. The music and the shouts and laughter of the other customers made it difficult to talk. And whether I wanted to think of him or not, Leonard's image was before me, life-size, persistent, almost tangible.

The last we'd *seen* of Leonard was two years ago on the night he came round to the apartment to show us some of his work, the way he often did. He liked the opinions of the unprejudiced, he said. He meant the uneducated and we let him get away with that. He came in wearing his usual scarecrow outfit, torn jeans and the grey-blue sweater his mother had knitted for him long ago. With his thin face and bony wrists, he looked like a starving artist which is what he was.

It's getting harder and harder for artists to starve as they once did but Leonard worked at it. He refused help from his parents who, in any case, didn't have much to spare. He'd turned down a job at McDonalds which would have given him food of a kind. And he depended on us for leftovers and encouragement. I felt sorry for him and at the same time I envied his dedication, his art.

Neither Jenny nor I had a date on that particular evening, and the other two rarely went out. I was wearing a black leotard and a flowered top that made me look like a medieval page boy. Or so I thought. It was what I changed into after I got home from work. Alice and Fran were still in their navy and black phase, darkly dressed in skirts and sweaters. Jenny, ever different, had on a long caftan in shades of green and brown and yellow and the gold slippers she'd bought in Turkey.

The cassette player was scratchily giving us an old Bob Dylan tune. *They ask me how I feel, And if my love is real.* His voice reminded us of a time before our time that we knew only as legend. None of us really believed in it but we liked to listen. The window was open to let the smell of broccoli soup drift out into the damp air.

Every time Leonard came to our place, he asked how the four of us could manage in that two-bedroom apartment without scratching each others eyes out. We had to be sensitive, that's all. We tried not stay in the shower too long or blame Alice for clogging the drains up with hair or leave sweaters to dry flat in the tub. It didn't always work.

Fran and Alice shared the larger bedroom. I had the other, a ten-by-ten box. Jenny slept on the fold-out couch in the living room which meant that she could have her player and books there and when she was ready for bed we all turned in. Or at least went quietly to our rooms. And I've since wondered if this arrangement wasn't getting on our nerves at that particular point in time. The point when Leonard came round to show us the last four drawings in his series: The pictures we all saw as our future selves etched out in shades of black and white and grey.

He was living in a studio with no running water on the third floor of a renovated factory on King Street. He wasn't supposed to sleep there but he did. He washed himself in the World's Best Donut restroom and came to us when he needed a shower. He washed his few clothes in the laundry room in the basement of our building. Usually he had to beg quarters from us to work the machines.

It was Alice who'd introduced Leonard to Jenny. She'd known him at high school. I could see them hanging around together, Alice and Leonard, a gangly boy and a chunky girl, neither jocks nor nerds, talking about life and art and groping towards sex. Leonard went on to art college but found the faculty old-fashioned, rigid and traditional. He quit. He met Alice again when he went to buy a pair of sneakers in the store where she worked. She was marking time there until her real vocation revealed itself.

Fran hated her job in the mall but it was experience; she planned to move on to catering or write a book about it. She'd served Alice a few times when Alice had lunch in the Food Hall, and had admired her long red hair. They'd argued about the sad sight of homeless people waiting to pick up leftovers. Fran thought they should be told to leave. Alice worried about them catching diseases. But before long, Fran had moved into the apartment too.

When I had, foolishly and wilfully according to my mother, decided to take a year off from university and come to the city to make my fortune, a phone call from her to my aunt landed me on Jenny's doorstep. The three of them made room for me and treated me kindly. To them I was Jenny's simple country cousin and, for a short time, I was their doll. Fran trimmed my hair. Alice lent me a white blouse. Jenny chose the colour of my lipstick. I went for six interviews and was offered a job on the bottom rung of the ladder in a company which made decorative window-blinds. We celebrated my achievement with brunch at Bright's Deli.

I planned to move to a place of my own as soon as I could. I desperately wanted to be able to watch the news every evening in peace. And I was tired of having to go to a pay phone every time I wanted to talk in private to the sociology professor who was breaking my heart.

It was 1980 and words like 'gloomy outlook,' 'near-recession' and 'jobs evaporate,' began to appear in the news. At work, the manager told me that since I was willing and cheerful, I would, should the need arise, get another job with no trouble. Jenny said that was the line they used when they were about to lay people off. The government had told them to employ encouraging phrases so as not to add plain human depression to the other kind. There were more people throwing themselves in front of subway trains than ever got into the papers. Why did I think it took so long to get back from work these evenings?

Jenny had stayed on at school, gone to Ryerson to get a diploma, and was working for a video company. They packaged and labelled videos and sent them all over the country. She talked about getting into production. There was going to be a revolution in technology and we should prepare for it. She always knew what was going on though I never once saw her read more of a newspaper than the horoscope and the cartoon about the two dogs. As a sideline, Jenny practised being rich. With so many of us sharing the rent, she could afford silk underwear. I think that's why she hadn't so far asked us to move out.

She'd been in love with Leonard for a short time but had been smart enough to dump him when she saw she might have to support him through twenty years of unbought artwork, critical neglect, stacked drawings everywhere and God forbid he should move on to oil. But every few days he came and showed us his stuff and we told him what we thought about it and let him help himself to whatever was in the fridge. It was habit, routine. Leonard was family.

He'd been working on a series of scenes of the city done in bars and outdoors and down Yonge Street, way down, in the centre of town. He aimed to have twenty-four of them and we'd already seen twenty and pronounced them to be first-rate.

I say way down Yonge Street because this apartment of Jenny's while it's near a subway station, it's the last subway station on the line, and once we get home at night we think twice before setting out again to some bar or concert. In fact, when I read the others that piece from *Time* about the new trend towards "cocooning," they knew exactly what it meant. We'd got into this comfortable habit of going into the building and pulling the drawbridge up after us, making a few calls, cooking up something and just staying home. We sat around listening to Jen's music, watching TV, or talking about the lousy situation regarding jobs and men.

So Leonard turned up about eight that one night with his portfolio and a look on his face that said, *I've got something really good here, guys.*

It could have been that he came in just then. At that moment. Maybe half an hour later, everything would've been different. And why did I get the idea that he wanted to go to bed with Jenny or with me? Just as a way of celebrating, a cheap way of celebrating the completion of his set of drawings.

My parents had come over from Scotland in the fifties. They'd taught me that while art itself was a good thing, artists were unreliable at best and bohemian at worst. I could see what they meant but definitely didn't agree. I rejected that along with all of their ideas about work and money and sex. But somewhere, deep down, was this feeling that an artist was a rogue, not to be trusted, and certainly not to be slept with. So when Leonard ran his hand over my shoulders as he walked by, I shook him off.

We'd been talking about the chances of Jenny's boss getting thrown out because he was neglecting his work to have long lunches with the head of packing, and what it would mean to Jenny if they both left. Jenny knew she could do both jobs standing on her head. And I wondered if when the vacancy came up and she moved on, there'd be a place for me. The market for decorative window blinds had hit an all-time low.

Fran was the only one of us who felt she had time. The rest of us had this feeling of life rushing by as if we were on one of those moving sidewalks and all the good jobs, good lovers and great parties were hurtling along much faster on either side of us. We could see it all but we were not getting any of it. Only Fran had a plan for her future and felt that it would work out. She was also the only one of us who ironed her jeans. I lived from hope to hope of better things just around the corner. Alice dreamed her way along, happy when Fran was happy, sad when Fran's schemes didn't include her. Jenny meanwhile worked with determination, grasping at opportunities, waiting to be lifted out of her lowly niche and brought to the top of the pyramid.

Alice had made her special salad for dinner to go with Fran's soup and we were sharing a bottle of wine, a Friday treat bought by Jenny because she was the lucky one who'd got a raise. It was all set to be one of our better evenings with stories and laughter and a mellow feeling all round.

But Fran was in a bad mood.

"I don't mind shopping for stuff," she suddenly shouted, "and cooking, but I want to find onions there when I need them and cheese and milk. If you eat it, replace it. OK!"

Alice looked guilty. Alice looked terminally guilty. I knew that she made extra sandwiches and gave them to a woman she worked with who was trying to bring up two kids on a part-time job.

Jenny said, "I'm tired. I don't need this."

Bob Dylan sang, "You're a big girl now."

"It happens all the time!"

I said to Fran, "Why don't you put a padlock on it?"

Fran told me to shut up.

Jenny said, "It's Leonard who takes the stuff."

I thought, He eats raw onions?

Then the buzzer rang. It seemed to ring exactly when Jenny mentioned his name but it was probably a few minutes later because, as I recall, Alice had cooled the atmosphere and was talking about shoes by the time he'd come up in the elevator and reached our door.

Anyway, enter Leonard with his portfolio. He went to the kitchen for a glass and poured the last of the wine into it. I'm not normally greedy but I'd been looking forward to half a glass more of that *Chablis*. It was five blocks to the liquor store and raining out and nothing takes the glow off the first glass of wine like having to go to the store to fetch the second.

And then he did what he usually did. He set up his scenes of city life around the room, one on the bookcase, one on the couch, and two leaning up against the wall. This time they were different. The others were general, crowds, buildings, traffic. These had single figures in them, figures with recognisable faces. He stood waiting, wanting our immediate attention.

But Alice wasn't a person who liked to be interrupted. She thought for a time before she spoke and then said slowly and carefully exactly what she wanted to say. She'd just said something like, "My manager says this new tax is going to ruin the shoe trade but I told him that people will always need shoes. They will, won't they?" and was waiting for a reply.

Fran said, "Maybe not so many pairs, honey."

Jenny said, "He needs to move into health shoes, heavy sandals. Things people think they need to keep their feet in shape."

Leonard coughed.

We got up and walked round to look at his work as if we were at one of those little galleries on Scollard and were about to stick red dots on his drawings.

I looked closely at the first sketch and saw Fran at work. She appeared to be distraught, her hair was all over the place, a dark stain bled down her uniform overall and one of her shoes untied. (Leonard had an eye for detail that didn't make him popular.) He'd emphasised her dark eyebrows and drawn in a double chin. She looked about sixty-years-old.

In the second one, Jenny was coming out of a theatre, her eyes closed, her hand on the arm of a man who wasn't at all her type. A small guy with a moustache and a mean smile. She was wearing what looked like a long fur coat, and boots.

In the park, the little park at the lower end of Jarvis it looked like, sat Alice, her hair flowing round her shoulders, a loose shapeless gown dripping to the ground. It was Spring in the park and the leaves were coming out, birds on branches, two drunks lying nearby. And Alice was sitting on a bench with her head back drinking from a small bottle shrouded in a paper bag.

He'd drawn me without a background. It was me against white, that was all. Me wearing my raincoat standing there expressionless against all that emptiness as if I had come from nothing and would return to nothing. Only down in the corner he had drawn a cat, shaded in black.

Leonard stood back as if he'd presented his drawings to a jury, or no, really, more as if he was presenting us with a great gift: These are your lives. This is what will become of you.

After a while, Alice said, "Crystal balls, Leonard!"

Jenny added, "Garbage, Leonard!"

Fran yelled, "I look to be about fifty there."

I said nothing because there was something terrifying about his picture of me that made me want to run back home to Welland and tell my parents they were right.

Leonard looked at us and at his pictures. He stood glancing from us to them, from them to us. Distress fell over his thin white face like one of our store's cheaper blinds. He finished his wine and left without saying goodnight and without the drawings.

For weeks we thought we heard him on the stairs or in the hall outside. We bought extra milk, left wine in the bottle and made sure there was the kind of cheese he liked in the fridge.

And then there was a postcard from Mexico, an Artists' Colony. It didn't say, *Wish you were here*. The message was incoherent. The word 'critic' was scrawled on it and some other words in Spanish we couldn't read.

We felt better after that. He was all right. We'd driven him to confront his art in a serious way.

Months later, another postcard arrived, this one from Los Angeles. It simply said, "They love me here."

So we fantasised about his life in the studios of the famous: He was painting backdrops for art movies, small cult films in which the details were noticed and recognised as part of the artistic whole. We went to the movies to look for his name among the credits but never found it.

It was Christmas when we got the letter. It was addressed to Jenny, written on paper headed, *Dean, Haverchuk and Dean, Chicago. Advertising to the nation.* He hoped we were all OK. He thought of us now and then. He was very busy but would be in Toronto soon and would buy us a beer, eh. He wasn't on the big accounts yet but any day would be moving up. He was drawing something that was to sell dried black bean soup to the eager, waiting world. He enclosed a sample package and hoped that we, his fondly remembered and earliest critics, would enjoy it.

We tipped the desiccated beans out onto the counter in the kitchen and stared at the brown dust for a while before we threw it out. We figured he would need all his talent to market the stuff.

"So the barman remembers him!"
    "He used to come in here and draw. You know."
    "Right."
    "Another round?"
    "Nothing for me."

◆

We had sometimes wondered if our comments that night had stopped Leonard from becoming an artist, a great and famous man with lots of money who would have made his parents proud and had his papers collected by the National Archive Library in Ottawa. Or if we'd saved him from starving to death in the street with his artistic soul intact.

Fran said, "A real artist would have kept on."

Jenny said, "He's got a good job."

Alice said, "We could have been kinder."

What I was thinking but didn't say aloud was that Leonard had taken something with him, a kind of hope. For the first year or so we'd waited for him to come back with new drawings, new outlines to change our lives for us. But after we saw the black bean flakes on the counter we knew we were on our own. He'd made his choice. We had to make ours. Those bean flakes had released us from all responsibility for Leonard. At the same time they let us know that we could expect nothing more from him.

"To Leonard," Fran said.

We held up our glasses and touched them across the table.

To Leonard, poor sucker! What did he know?

None of us spoke for a moment, then Jenny said, "I bet he's making scads of money."

I said to Jenny, "I'll be moving out soon. Soon as I get a full-time job."

Jenny put her hand on mine and whispered, "It's all right."

Any moment we were going to leave that bar with its cheerful noise and loud people and walk out into a street full of traffic and strangers and go back to Jenny's and curl ourselves up small to fit into the apartment which was crowded with our clothes and books and boxes. We'd watch TV and I'd have to sit on the cushion on the floor as usual.

I got up and walked away from our table. There were tears on my face for no reason at all except that I wanted Leonard to come back and draw me a life. But more than anything in the entire world just then, I wanted a cat of my own.

LIFE DRAWING

Tibbles turned ten today. It sounds like a kids' poem or the beginning of a book. It's only remarkable because it took me ten years after I left Jenny's to get a cat and then ten more to realise that black cats are lucky. No, I'm not going to arrange a little kitty party. I have moved on. There was a time when I would have put candles on a tiny salmon pie and singed the poor thing's whiskers trying to get it to blow them out. Cats resent that kind of thing and no one needs a resentful cat about the place. So Tibbles gets sardines and I get to go out for a dinner which will begin with wine, move on to an argument about the health service and end up with 'sexual congress.' Connor used that phrase on the phone yesterday. He's been in politics too long.

I have a few hours to spare. This is so rare these days that it feels like a vacation. No appointments. No speech to prepare. I've taken the Mahler disc out of the player and put on Beethoven's *Pastoral*. The phone is on call-answer and I won't respond to it. I want to think about last night which means thinking about my life.

We didn't meet in the old bar yesterday. It was torn down several years ago. We met in the glossy new place on Gloucester. Jenny chose it. It was her turn to pay for our annual get-together. My wealthy cousin can afford these things. So can I but I have to be careful where I'm seen to be spending the taxpayer's money.

Tibbles's basket is ready for the long drive tomorrow. He senses when it's time for us to take off again. Sees me tidying the apartment, packing my suits and papers. In bad weather we go by train. Flying gives him hysterics.

Alice was the first to arrive at *La Jarrie*. When I got there, she had already ordered a bottle of *Pouilly-Fuissé* and was fingering the silverware like a thief. She was wearing a loose black garment with an orange design and Hallowe'en make-up. After she left the shoe business, she'd also quit aerobics. She looked largely lovely. I said so. She poured me a glass of wine and told me I looked every bit a superwoman. A compliment? Perhaps not.

"Before the others get here."

I sensed danger and didn't respond.

"I don't know how you do what you do," she said. "You're so easy to read. I'm not looking for a parking ticket fix. I don't want a loan. I just want to tell you about Fran."

Fran had moved over to the other side. For six months she'd been seeing a man called Jason who didn't care about her past. Alice cared. Even though she and Fran hadn't been a couple for years, it was a betrayal.

"She's not happy," Alice said. "He's in it for the freak show aspect. I happen to know that he's been overheard at the gym saying 'I'm fucking this lesbian and it's great.'"

"You should keep that to yourself," I said.

"Oh ho. Miss Prim."

"Fran is here."

Fran was way beyond her slovenly, anything-goes years. Her pantsuit was sleek-fitting charcoal with a hint of gold. She walked towards us holding a menu she'd snatched from the desk. She couldn't wait for the one already at her place on the table.

"These can't be fresh," she said of the fiddleheads. "Be wary of the sea-bass. It won't be the real thing. The veal should be properly cooked here. If not, send it back."

Alice said, "Lovely to see you, Fran. You've heard about Jenny and Peter?"

But just then, Jenny came towards us escorted by the cod-faced maitre d'. Exotic, assured, she looked worth every penny of the Hoffman wealth. I didn't want to hear what Alice had to say. I wanted Jenny to be happy. I wanted to know that her children had loving and close parents who would never argue and never go their separate ways. And Jenny, as she sat down, did as she had done when we were three lonely, impecunious twenty-year-olds. She made us welcome in her space.

"What can I get you to drink, ladies?" the waiter asked.

Alice didn't bother to berate him for not saying 'women,' she ordered a second bottle and said it might be a three-bottle night, maybe four. After two glasses, she stopped glancing towards the window as if all the homeless people in Toronto were pressing their faces to the glass and pointing at her.

Jenny whispered to me, "I've heard."

I said, "It's not confirmed."

But it was going to be. I had assurances from the top.

My grown-up life, theirs too, had only begun when the four of us were smoked out of the old apartment building at Jane and Finch and had to look for other places to live. We'd been snug there, trapped in our routines as if we might grow old together and remain what we were until retirement: shoe salesperson, fast food server, video packager, blind-maker.

God knows how long we'd have stayed in that nest if the convenient fire hadn't made it possible for the landlord to put the place on the market.

Jenny fell in love. Alice went crazy. Fran took a serious cookery course. I wept because I couldn't afford to live in the city on my own. I did what a lot of people do in that situation, I went home to my parents. Failure was written on my skin plainly for everyone to see. Desperate to get me out of the house where my main occupation was moping, my Dad introduced me to Frank. Frank walked up and down with me beside the murky canal and said, "We have to do something about this."

◆

The wild mushroom soup the waiter set down in front of me, reminded me of what the canal looked like then.

"It's disgusting," I said aloud.

The others looked at me and I told them I was thinking of the Opposition's attitude to welfare. But I was still on the path beside the canal with Frank and that's what I'd said to him. *It's disgusting!* And Frank had stopped me then and told me there was a great deal to be done and I must be part of it.

When a reporter asks me now how I got my start, I'm tempted to say, *In dirty water.* But circumspect is my middle name. It has to be. The members of the press pounce on every word. It's better to throw them a few small sins now and then in the hope that they never discover the big one.

Jenny brought out photographs of her children. Kelsey was growing to look more and more like her as she was when we all lived together. Charlie had his father's look of determined optimism. The world will treat Charlie well. We asked about their health and education like fond aunties.

Shortly after I'd gone back home, the blind business boomed along with housing prices. I found later that the company had tried to get hold of me to re-hire me, even to offer me more money. They didn't find me. Was this fate? Or was it simply that Welland is off most people's map of Canada?

◆

The waiter had taken the entree plates back to the kitchen along with Fran's comments about the oil the chef had used to cook the frites before any of us mentioned black bean flakes.

Fran said, "So, Leonard, eh?" We smiled at each other in a self-congratulatory way as if we'd been responsible for his success. I suppose it was fair to think he might have starved in those years without our leftovers.

"So tell us, Janice," Alice said. "Who's going to win this time?"

"It's a foregone," Fran said. "The economy's good. There's a chicken in every pot."

"The people I deal with don't have pots," Alice stated.

"Well in most pots. Not always very well cooked. The things people do to good chickens should come up at the Human Rights Commission."

"Let her speak."

"She was always the quiet one," Jenny said. "And now we're hanging on her words."

"It's not so much the undecideds who'll count this time," I said. "It's the switchers. That small group of people who wait and see which candidate they prefer. The switchers don't vote party, they vote policy. They're a bugbear to pollsters, to everybody."

"Sounds to me like they're honest and sensible."

"If you like," I replied. "But you could think about the Vicar of Bray."

"All that reading she did in the library."

"You don't want me to sing in here."

"So who was he?"

"Just a man who changed his principles to keep in with whoever was in power."

◆

Walking by the canal, Frank talked about the Irish labourers who'd built it. About the number of different languages spoken in the small area around this piece of man-made water that linked the great lakes. Then he said I had to come and work in his office. My Dad knew what he was about.

"But you're talking about the ordinary man and woman who have nothing to gain," Jenny said.

"Logically, yes."

"I'm going to vote NDP. No question," Alice said. "They care."

"They haven't a hope. And it's taking votes away."

"Nothing would ever change on that basis. No other party would have a chance."

"They've had a chance."

Frank got me onto joe jobs at first. Sticking up posters, filling envelopes and, finally, researching facts and re-writing speeches.

"So what's your lot going to do about tax. This is the highest taxed country in the Western world."

"No it's not," I said. I'd known they would begin to peck at me after a while. "Other countries have hidden taxes. Ours are overt."

"Whatever," Fran said. "They're too fucking high.

I've got to pay all the benefits for my staff. You've increased minimum wage. My dishwashers can afford vacations in Hawaii."

"Good," said Alice.

"Hey," Jenny said. "Let's leave politics out of this, OK."

"We don't often get to sit down with a live one and find out what's really going on in Ottawa," Alice answered. "So, listen, Janice, are you really sleeping with that guy who donates all that money to the party?"

There was more laughter.

Jenny said, "Peter wants to know what you're going to do about the Kurds."

"This isn't the States" Fran said. "What power do we have? Anyway, what can she do."

"What's Peter's interest?"

"Ha! The politician's question. What's in it for him?"

Not long after our walk by the canal, I found out what was in it for Frank: Me.

"Don't you believe in philanthropy?"

"Is it philanthropy if you get a whopping tax write-off?"

"The old argument. It's only good if it hurts?"

"Come on, girls, we're here to have fun."

I licked dozens of envelopes in that office in Welland before they gave me a moist sponge to save my tongue.

I read speeches and edited them and began to write them myself. I came to the notice of the local MP. When you become good at something, even a small thing like sticking stamps on straight or taking adverbs out of an address to the Rotary Club, it gives you the confidence to move on. Gradually I put mousiness behind me, became smart, and was asked to move to Head Office. In bed one night before I left Welland, Frank said, "I'll miss you."

"Your wife won't," I answered.

Soon after that evening long ago, the evening when Leonard had come round to the apartment to ask our opinions on his latest work, Jenny and Fran and Alice had angrily thrown his drawings out. I'd kept mine in the bottom of my underwear drawer and taken it with me from the apartment to Welland, to Toronto, to Ottawa where I keep it.

When I first looked at the picture and saw that he'd drawn me and a cat small against a background of white, I'd felt afraid. All that whiteness was a cell in the madhouse, a life of eternal nothingness which lay ahead. For years, I dreaded my own blank future.

I know now that what Leonard had shown me was a tabula rasa. I was unformed, that's what he was telling me. I could do anything; it was up to me.

They were lifting their glasses.

Jenny said, "Here's to Janice."

And I was simpering in the way I try not to, aiming for dignity and trying not to cry.

I never told Frank about the girl. The girl I called Lenny, and gave away.

We walked out through the dining room with its crystal and flowers and white napery. Other diners turned to look at us and maybe in the dim light recognised the charity organiser, the restaurateur, the woman who works among the desperate, or the politician.

Out on the street, we looked at each other as we always do before we part for another year. Like the survivors of a shipwreck, we check in now and then to make sure the others are hanging on to the lifeboat, heads above water. It could be curiosity that binds us together. Or maybe it's love. Anyway, we've celebrated another year of life, four lives. *See you next year.*

I'll wear my navy underwear to have dinner with Connor tonight. And over it, the off-turquoise suit I bought in New York. It's the colour of the moment. We'll come back to my place later. We'll have a drink. He'll comment on the white walls, the starkness of the apartment, and the blackness of the cat that sits in the corner.

THE HAROLD SEQUENCE

CHURCH

Nine

*Well! and what if she should die
some afternoon . . .*

—T.S. ELIOT, "PORTRAIT OF A LADY"

When Harold Fryer went to church that August Sunday, he had to begin by reminding God of his existence. As a boy he had sung *Jesus loves me* often enough to believe he was known up there in the sky among the clouds and angels. Once when he was about eleven, he had seen a vision of the Christ child in colour on his bedroom wall. But at twelve he had lost religion and learnt to blow frogs apart with firecrackers. Now, thirty years later, he needed to renew the policy and wasn't sure how to go about it.

As he went up the church steps on his own, he murmured, "Hi! I'm Harold Fryer." There was no response. He didn't really expect God to lean down and say, *Well am I ever glad to see you, Hank,* or even, *Where the hell've you been?* but he would have liked to feel a touch on his shoulder, a reassuring puff of holy breath on his cheek, a sudden warm glow as he reached the top step. And there was nothing! At least the All-Seeing hadn't given him a shove and pushed him down the steps and into the street.

He was here because premiums must be paid in advance. Right! A rule. A fact of accident and life. A matter of common sense. There is no such thing as insurance after the event. Fires and accidents can't or shouldn't be foreseen. *Mine is not a morbid occupation*, he said to those who asked. It's life-enhancing work. It gives comfort and provides a cushion, emotional ease to men and women whose lives are often stressed enough without them having to worry about fire and flood.

All his working life, not counting the stretch at Happy Hamburger and two summers re-surfacing roads, he had gone into rooms with his hand outstretched saying, *Hi, I'm Harold Fryer and I'm with Midway Insurance.*

"Tell people your name, what you do, make yourself clear to them right off the bat. Start out straight," his first manager, old Crowley, had said as if after that he could make any crooked turns he liked.

He'd left Betty at home getting ready for their trip, listening to the radio, to a memorial concert for a singer he'd never liked. Once when their talk had briefly gone beyond the day-to-day, Betty had told him she knew Marlene Dietrich would have understood her. And he, laughing, had replied that all the star understood was sex and money. Looking back now he could see that was the wrong response. She had cried then. But the tears on her cheeks this morning were as much for her dad killed in the war as for the singer or for any of the usual reasons.

Harold stepped inside the church nodding to the ones he knew. A few of his customers were there taking out a different kind of policy on life, insuring themselves for afterwards, if there was an afterwards, though in this place it was wise to suppress all doubt. Some of them responded to his nod with the specially bright smiles of the saved, pleased to welcome him, the sinner, to the lowest rung of the ladder.

I took the straight option, he informed God as music engulfed the church and a smattering of feet on tile told him the service was about to begin. Under the music he heard his own thought repeated over and over: *I loved her as she set out on the water.*

He had expected the church to feel more homelike. The church of his boyhood had been as much bakeshop as House of God with the women all the time having sales and brewing up potluck suppers and strawberry teas. His dad had quit going because he said that whatever the time of year the damn church smelled like Thanksgiving. His mother had replied it was no call to turn heathen but his dad said he wanted to spend his one day off weeding the garden and if heaven was going to reek of turkey then he'd prefer to spend eternity elsewhere, thank you very much.

There was a shuffling all around and he knelt in his pew and said without speaking, "Hi, I'm Harold Fryer. Remember me? I know it's been a time."

Voices in unison murmured responses he had long forgotten and covered the words that crowded into his head.

This evening, people will be making their way back to the city. We'll have privacy, Betty. You know how quiet it is.

Well I'd like quiet.

Meet me outside the church in an hour.

This church smelled of cheap floor polish. It was stark, modern. Its pillars were wooden masts, its walls were blocks, its windows coloured glass; no patterns, no stories told in large mosaic tiles. There were just a few wooden boards on the walls dedicated to special people. To Glenda Warbin for courageous service. To certain soldiers killed young. To benefactors.

Standing up to sing, the people began to work their way into "The Lord's my shepherd." He remembered the words but they were singing them to a different tune.

He tried to follow with "I shall not want. He leadeth me. He leadeth me beside," but they got ahead and lost him. And he could still hear in his head the words of the pagan song that had followed him from the house that morning: *Who'd want to cry when he says goodbye to a sweetheart . . .*

It was cold, this church, like the one they were married in. He'd hardly noticed the building that day, full as it was with lace and hats and relatives and his sisters in flouncy blue gowns. There had been an altar and a tapestry behind it with woven figures of men fishing. He'd kept his eye on that and tried to remember his lines. IdoIdoIdoIdoIdon't. *Meet me at the church at noon, Betty.*

"You've got a good one there," his dad had said at the reception. But neither of them noticed that under the wing of dark hair, the bride's mouth turned down and her eyes could darken in seconds like a storm getting up over a lake. And how suddenly she could become silent. Silent like water after rain, like water closing over a head.

You need insurance, Mrs. Belchuk. Insurance helps you sleep easy at night, lets you know that whatever disaster happens, you're not going to be out on the street. Things happen when you least expect. Midway takes care of its customers. And I will take care of you.

Harold had never lived in dangerous countries or known how to starve or lie behind rocks and shoot at people who might have been his brothers or neighbours. He'd never even damaged the car and fire had not eaten up his belongings and left him homeless. Burglars stayed away from his house. So surely he was a good risk. *Just this one thing, Almighty Shepherd.*

The music stopped. All around him, people were listening carefully to the words of the lesson as if He could really see the sparrow fall and the hungry man weep and the woman drown.

Harold recalled some tale from long ago about a woman drowning in her own tears, and in a way that's what Betty had done. When her face came to him in nightmares now, it was through streaks of water like a rainy day through glass.

A gathering of boys and girls, knowing sweet nothing, lifted their voices to holler Alleluia. And then sang words in such a high key that they hurt his ears.

Insure against flooding, Mrs. Belchuk. Rare in this area but not unknown. Call it water damage. I've seen a piano ruined, books destroyed, wallpaper down in shreds. The premiums are nothing compared to the peace of mind I am offering you.

The terms coming through to him in this place were similar to his own, familiar, reassuring. Be not afraid, you are insured with the best. We stand by our policies.

As long as you have paid in time.

On their wedding night Betty had said gleefully—there had been pleasure then—*What have you done, Harold Fryer?* When he had sold their house and bought their so-much-easier-to-care-for condo, she had said it again in a very different tone. And had begun to cry. And had not stopped since. Three years of crying, Lord, he said remembering the right title. Lord, how she has cried.

The clergyman in his modern brief pulpit leaned down and looked directly at Harold, and said, "I have taken as my text, 'The foolish body hath said in his heart, there is no God.'"

He was going to talk about casting them into the fiery furnace. Harry could feel it coming on. He wished he had with him the old illustrated prayer book that had given him comfort in similar times long ago with its pictures of lambs and gentle women in blue and white. But being a modern man, this priest began to talk wilderness and left hell to the imagination. Hell was local. Hell was custom-made. Hell was another person.

Who'd want to cry when he says goodbye to one sweetheart, since another is waiting round the next corner.

He could see Betty now in the meeting with the lawyer when they were selling the house, and it had sprung out at him how she would always set up an alliance with the other one. He hated the way she did that when they were in an office or wherever. Almost right away. She would do it now if she were here in Church with him. She would be nodding at the Lord, saying little asides: *Well yes, poor Harry, always been colour blind, always had a problem, talks too much, doesn't know about values, supposed to be so smart. Take no notice of him, God!*

The preacher went on, "Nothing is hidden. God who is inside each of us, like a scanner, knows . . . "

By the lake, they would say, seeing him there, white, splashed, silent, *Give him hot strong coffee. Get him away. He shouldn't see this. It's terrible. Poor man. He's in shock. Keep him warm. Make him lie down. The police will want to talk to him.*

Hi, my name is Harold Fryer. My mother wanted me to be a doctor but I sell insurance. It is not such a life-threatening job. Your future is my future, Mrs. Belchuk.

We know this is a terrible blow, Mr. Fryer, but there are some questions.

"And like a scanner, reading not only the thoughts and plans but also the excuses, the reasons we give to ourselves when we are about . . . "

Why was your wife out in the boat alone?

Did you know she had set out?

The weather is sudden on this lake.

Hi my name is Harold Fryer.

Were you a devoted couple?

Did you know that your boat had a split seam?

Had you been heard to say you were going to caulk it next time at the lake?

You didn't prevent her from going?

My name is Harold Fryer.

You didn't prevent her from going!

She was a wilful woman.

Water had become the centre of their lives. She talked and cried. He boiled water for tea. *Drink this, dear. I'd be happy if I could, Harold. A warm bath is soothing. Why can't we afford a Jacuzzi? Or go to the sea? A week by the lake, at the cottage. Take the canoe. I want to stay at a lodge. Not be cooking and cleaning. What kind of a break is that for me? The cottage has all mod cons, honey. And my sisters were just there. It'll be clean.*

The canoe was tied to the top of the car all ready for the journey. That evening they would settle in. For all her sorrow she packed food that was good, fruit, cheese, bread, soft drinks.

Neither of us drinks alcohol, Lord/sergeant.

First it was because we couldn't afford it. Then we saw what it did to our friends.

She takes the canoe out in the sober morning.

Go on Betty, go on. You used to be a whizz at it.

She smiles and is cheered by the sight of rocks and pines.

I could have been happy here.

Take the paddle. Go on. I'll watch.

Won't you come with me?

We can't change our lives now, honey.

He had customers who liked him, who depended on him. He had Francie and didn't want to lose her. Francie had laughter where Betty had tears. Francie knew delight.

And Francie needed his love. He needed hers. Francie was the only person who called him *Harry.*

Was your wife well insured?

Naturally.

For a large sum?

Fifty thousand dollars is not more than you might win in a lottery any weekend, eh Lord?

But there had to be an accounting. No one knew

more about audits and bottom lines than he did. Payments came due and the balance had to be kept straight. He'd taken out insurance on his life at a good price years ago. Prudently. Prudently. Betty, in the event of his death, provided for. And now here he was taking out an all-inclusive for his soul.

He saw her getting up pleased next morning, smiling, commenting on the trees, the shimmer on the lake, the cool clean air. She would go out alone but was a little scared, a little held-back. It was, for her, a definite act, something she had to do to prove that there would be fewer tears in future. He would look at her lovingly, loving her less as her toes touched the water and she drew her foot back in a silly shrieking way. She wasn't young, after all.

Take the canoe, sweetheart. Go on. Go on.

The guy up front there, wrapped in white, had spent his life going up to people saying, Hi, I'm Michael, your friendly priest, my insurance policies cost nothing, only every Sunday of your life and some weekdays and a voluntary contribution. In return you get a time-share in paradise. Cheap at twice the price.

His voice was drawing them to a close. *Now let thy servants depart.* Organ notes poured out and rose higher and filled up the space, driving the congregation away, making them hurry to the door.

God knows he knows the boat is a touch weak but no one is asking her to stand up out there and tip the boat over. He is only waving. She has no need to wave back.

The breeze came up from nowhere, sergeant.

As he walked out of the church, he said to the waiting priest, "Hi my name is Harold Fryer."

And the priest, young in his black and white outfit, aware of evil but knowing nothing of its reality, replied, "I know."

Harold, startled, stepped back almost falling down the stone steps. The clergyman reached out to hold his arm. Smiled at him, became his saviour. And Harold knew. He saw now, as he stood there, all of it, the plan, the intervention from above. In detective stories they said to watch for that moment when the ordinary man does something out of character. *You went to church Harry Fryer,* a thousand accusing voices shouted at him, screeching like crows, *for the first time in twenty years!*

"You sold me my first policy," the priest said.

"Ah. Yes." Harold replied but it was too late.

Fear had struck at his soul like a cold steel knife.

In that moment he knew that he was known. All his thoughts, the half-formed plans were visible. Bloody murder was written on his brow for all to see.

Francie Francie Francie Francie, he cried out silently, bitterly, feeling tears on his own face as he ran down the steps.

He said softly, "I was only going to tell my wife the truth." And was unheard against the noise of traffic.

In the parking lot by the hatchback, there was Betty, make-up covering the sad skin under her eyes, trying to smile as she secured the rope that tied the canoe to the top of the car. She was wearing her blue and grey leisure outfit, waiting for him to drive her to the vacation that was to solve all their problems. His and hers. He held the door open for her and walked round and got into the car beside her.

"I think it's going to be a dry week," she said.

"Let's hope so, honey," Harold replied as he turned the car towards the North. "Let's hope so."

THE COTTAGE

"Nelly, do you never dream
queer dreams?" she said, suddenly,
after some minutes reflection.

—EMILY BRONTE

As I pulled onto the grass beside our family's old cottage, Greta came out to greet me. Lorne appeared behind her. There was a tiptoeing, whispering feel to the welcome that mystified me till I followed them inside and saw Janine perched on the old couch with her feet up, reading. She glanced up from her book and nodded.

Worse still, a strange man was standing at the kitchen counter chopping young green things and putting them into a bowl. When he saw me, he turned with a kindly smile and raised his wet hands to show he would have embraced me if he could.

"I'm Sean, Annie," he said.

"Was the traffic bad?" Greta asked.

"Yes."

"Lovely to see you."

"Lovely to be here."

I'd driven north recalling days spent splashing around in the lake, me and Greta and the Fryer kids. Evening games of Monopoly and Hearts. Great times. I'd arrived almost prepared to enjoy the weekend. Now

I wanted to turn round and head straight back to the city.

"Lorne will get you a drink in a minute. Won't you, Lorne?"

Lorne carried my bag through to the closet behind the living room and apologised for the makeshift bed. I waited for him to say something like, *I realise this could be a little awkward, Annie.*

But he simply said, "You'll be all right on this bed. Martin slept on it last time he was here. Janine and her friend—kind of a surprise visit."

"Fine," I said.

I hung up my city clothes behind the door and put on my cottage outfit, jeans and T-shirt. I wanted to shout out, *what the hell is she doing here?*

Janine had been Lorne's secret love of four years before; a hot city passion of lunches and afternoons in a place on Prior Street which was discreet and out of sight but not far enough out of sight. A kind friend had told Greta. There had been a row. Forgiveness. Exit Janine bitterly on a golden broomstick.

Drinks were brought and the five of us sat on garden chairs in a row on the deck. Lorne was at the right, then Janine, then Sean, then my sister, then me. Greta drew our attention to the leaves and said it was only the middle of August. Coppery red had burnt into the green of the maples, and the birches were taking on a yellowish tinge. It had been a dry summer. We were all drinking rum and coke except for Janine who had asked for red wine. Behind us the white wall of the cottage reflected heat. In front of us, out on the lake, a loon laughed.

There was no sign of life in the cottages on either side. Since the old man died three years ago, there'd been no more family get-togethers at the Fryers' place. Fiona and Eleanor came up in spring and fall to clean it. Harold and his wife spent their vacations elsewhere. Betty had told Greta that she hated the place; it was dingy, inconvenient, hard work. The other cottage was up for sale. The Flugels were divorced and had no happy memories to draw them back.

Lorne said, "Annie loves the city. It's all we can do to pry her loose from there two or three times a year."

Janine said, "This is a heavenly place. I had no idea it was like this, Lorne."

She spoke with soft intimacy as if he and she had discussed it often and he had shown her photographs and she was here to take over. Janine moved with the gestures of a heavy woman who thought herself thin. She turned her profile to the lake, raised and lowered her left foot, and grasped the stem of her glass with two fingers and her thumb. I inhaled the special scent of pine and brush.

We had another drink. By this time, several more leaves had turned red. Lorne had tilted his chair forward to look down at a rock with a line of quartz in it. Greta had bunched her hair on to the top of her head and was holding it there. Sean stared at the island. The loon cried out again. I wanted to know what was for dinner and who was going to cook it.

Sean began to speak of Nature and her wonderful effect on fretful humours, on crazed city-dwellers who raced about in frantic pursuit of useless goals and worthless prizes.

"It is," he said, "an absence of green which causes stress. Look at Annie's face. See how, as she sits here, her facial muscles are beginning to relax."

"That's the rum," Lorne said. He spent too much time with his first-year students and shared their level of wit.

Greta said she had almost been called in to work but another nurse had volunteered. Janine turned her other profile to the lake. Even though she was about fifteen pounds overweight, she had a kind of dry elegance. Maybe it was her look of quiet melancholy which Lorne had found irresistible. I sat there drinking fast, thinking up some crisis at the office which might take me back to town on a weekend. I wondered how, if he was so clever, Sean couldn't tell the difference between relaxed muscles and a face rapidly setting into a mask of aggression.

I said to Greta, "Can I help with dinner?"

The usual idea that people who live alone eat randomly out of cans and packages doesn't apply to me. When I'm home, I make a planned dinner for around seven. I set a place with my Swedish flatware, a fine glass, and lace mats as if I were expecting my mother or her sisters. Only the music is different.

Greta didn't seem to have heard, so I said again, "Is there anything I can do about dinner?"

Sean replied for her. "See, the city is still in there. Ms. Annie can't enjoy this feast for the eyes because the body wants its fix. Relax. Spell it. R-E."

Lorne in an unusually high voice broke in to say, "Sean is a potter. He drove Janine here from the Soo."

Janine acknowledged this with her thin smile. I wanted to ask if she'd taken a vow of silence.

Sean launched into one of those monologues that cottage decks bring out of people in the early evening. As he talked, Lorne fidgeted, tugging at the hem of his green shorts as if he wanted to make them into slacks to cover his hairy legs. I looked back twenty years and recalled how, in my teens, I used to be bored with cottage country by August, and would count off the days till school started again.

"I used to be a lawyer, Annie. Used to find accident victims and say, *you're hurt, you need a lawyer*. Not, you know, in an aggressive sort of way. To be helpful. To make sure they were aware of what their rights were. One day, snow was coming down like thick showers of flaked coconut, and this guy got hit from behind so hard his head went through the roof of the car."

He stopped for a moment and looked as though he was going to cry. "I was there. I live with it every day of my life. I was the guy who hit him."

Greta said, "Sean brought us a pot."

Janine said, "Vase."

I said, "Was he killed?"

Sean said, "Decapitated."

Lorne said, "The rocks over there are a fine example of Precambrian."

I looked at his lined and craggy face and wondered how he could behave in such a Neanderthal way. How could he have allowed this to happen? When Greta had forgiven him for the affair, I had too. My old fondness for him had returned; he was reliable, kind Lorne again. And now, here was Janine sitting with us like an erratic on a prairie!

Greta got up and went into the kitchen. As I stood

up to follow, Sean, like a master of ceremonies, waved me back to my chair and followed Greta himself. I moved across the gap and sat next to the other two. Janine stared at me wishing me elsewhere but I stayed on answering Lorne's questions about his software until we were called to dinner.

Sean had whisked up a dressing with sesame seeds and oil for his organic salad. Greta had thawed out a dish of lasagne which had hardened as it re-heated. We sat there and chewed. Sean talked about the change in his lifestyle, and Lorne made philosophical comments that sounded as though they were out of a book called, four hundred ways to change your life without really trying.

Finally I said to Janine, "Are you staying long?"

Lorne choked on a hard crumb of noodle.

Janine replied in a voice that was like a shallow stream running over pebbles.

"Annie. Is it anything to you how long I stay? I've told Greta and Lorne that I'm passing through. I'm also passing through a very difficult time in my life."

"I'm sorry," I said.

"Sean and I both have our problems to deal with."

And you've come to dump them on my sister?

"He drove my car all the way here, very kindly. And I thought a day or two in this lovely place would do him good."

"I see."

"I'm not sure that you do."

She'd always suspected me of being the one who'd spied on her and Lorne and betrayed them to Greta.

"Sometimes," she said, "it's a matter of moving on,

moving into another space. Considering options. Taking control."

It seemed to me that she was expecting a lot to come out of one weekend.

She took a breath and we all waited. And then she turned to me with a sweet smile and said, "So how long are you staying?"

"As long as it takes," I said.

Greta had been on the point of going to the kitchen to fetch a dish of fruit salad but sat still.

Lorne said, "More wine?"

Janine continued, "Sean was like me, somewhat on the peak. At the peak of his profession, his powers. Until . . ."

Lorne spilled wine on the tablecloth and we all tried to help out with paper towels, salt, water. Sean said that salt worked on blood not wine. And I wondered why Greta was using old family linen at the cottage for Chrissake. Then I saw, as she dabbed at it, that she'd brought it out as a desperate gesture, a talisman perhaps, something old to protect her from an unknown evil.

After dinner we sat outside again, Lorne at the left, then Janine, then Greta, then me, then Sean. In the background was a medley of panpipe music which Sean had brought with him and which was supposed to calm our inner souls. I wished I was sitting on my tiny balcony listening to the sound of the city, thinking of next morning's run, of meeting Tom and Marcie and Dave in Gerry's bar and talking over our options in the upcoming merger.

Greta whispered to me, "I'll come to your room later on."

Lorne on his way out of the kitchen had murmured, "We have to talk."

Mosquitoes were biting my ankles. Sean told me in a thousand words to Zen it out.

"When I was still a lawyer," Sean went on as if he was Daddy telling a bedtime story to the children, "I used to think that a good deal of crap mattered which doesn't."

Amazing insight!

"I would get into these relationships and arguments and it was the end of the world when it was over but you know how it is. The world kept turning. Life went on. Work was there. Life was there. Nature was there. Think of that, Annie. You are a mere flea on the world's underbelly."

Greta got up muttering, "Coffee, more coffee," and went into the kitchen.

I turned and hit Sean on the side of the head. He looked at me in stunned sorrow.

"You were asking for that," I said.

Lorne said, "Annie! What's gotten into you."

Janine's mouth was one round o.

Sean, holding his cheek, began to speak.

"Don't start," I warned him.

And I followed Greta into the kitchen and turned the cassette player off.

"What is all this? Who is that freak? And why is she here?"

Greta reached for a jar from the shelf and didn't answer. I touched her shoulder.

"Tell me," I said.

"I wanted to call and tell you to take a rain check

but Lorne was insistent. Really insisted. No need to disappoint you, he said. And it's Labour Day in two weeks. There might not be another chance this summer."

"I like sleeping in the closet!"

"Anyway she's here."

"You don't get a lot of time off."

"I'm all right. The affair's long over. I'm fine."

Her voice was brittle, challenging.

I could see Janine out there on the deck beside Lorne, a monument of silent possession, holding his hand, taking in the landscape. I set my back against the window and watched Greta grinding coffee beans.

"But who is he?" I asked.

"He's a friend. Of hers. She brought him to do the driving. Don't let him get to you. He's on his way to Toronto. He wants to drive back with you."

"My car only holds one."

Greta was wearing an old pair of grey slacks and a loose top. She looked bedraggled, slight, and less of a sister to me than a daughter. In that moment, she was totally without any kind of defence, unaware or denying that she had been invaded. Like the old pirate stories she'd loved as a kid, she had been boarded by the enemy. Seized. Taken. And could easily be made to walk the plank. The lake out there in the evening light was sinister.

Lorne came into the kitchen in a what-are-you-two-girls-up-to way, smiling his dark smile, tall, stooping, all charm and love. So Lorne had insisted that I come, had he? Good old Lorne!

"Lorne," I said.

"Not a word. I'm going to make my special coffee."

"Don't you think we've all had enough?"

"Take her outside, Greta. Let this city sister of yours enjoy the view. Tell her to relax. R,E, etcetera."

Greta stood on tiptoe to kiss him as if admiring his hospitable ways.

Sean had moved to Lorne's chair and was sitting next to Janine and pointing to the edges of the lake. Soon there would be stars. And he would know the name of every last one. He stood up to give me a hug of forgiveness and I was too startled to stop him.

Janine said, "Tomorrow we can go out in the canoe, Lorne said."

"All five of us?" I asked.

"Well, four of us. I guess it only holds four."

I slept badly. It was hot and a mosquito had got into the closet. I missed my fan and my own bed and the smoky air of my street and the siren sounds of the local guardians of peace and well-being. Instead I could hear footsteps and whispers and scrabbling animals.

I woke from a nightmare: An image of Greta, her hair floating like weeds on the surface of that dark lake, had entered the cottage and swelled up to fill it with a sense of treachery and doom. My open eyes met pitch darkness. I lay awake not wanting to return to the ugly dream. Morning was a long time coming.

In the kitchen, Lorne was insisting that Greta must come in the canoe with him and Sean and Janine.

Janine, with a new liveliness, was pushing at Greta to make her fetch her lifejacket. Sean was standing by the door like an impatient adventurer. Greta wanted to stay in and tidy up, she said, but was weakening, ready to give in.

I played dumb and put on my sunhat and a ton of sunscreen and ignored the suggestion that I should stay behind and let Greta go. Sean then offered strongly to stay. But I shouted him down. I said that if Greta wanted to stay behind, she should be allowed to. Maybe she wanted a little time on her own and didn't he take a lot on himself, organising people's lives for them.

Was it the gloomy green of the pines, the impossible depth of the lake, the unknown creatures lurking there among the rocks that had brought on my nightmare? The image of Greta dragging under the water was so strong that I would have knocked her out rather than let her go in that canoe with the other three that morning.

We filed down to the lake, Lorne, then me, then Janine, then Sean. Lorne handed me a paddle and took the centre place in the small green boat. I sat in the stern, Sean and Janine in the bow.

Janine looked angrily at me and turned silent and we pulled out onto the lake and I stared at my brother-in-law's face: Lorne. Lover. Loverlorne. Playing a game of his own. Playing now at silent Indian moving over mysterious water.

We glided through scenery that has been painted in oil and watercolour and hung in every gallery in Canada. Relentless pines and rocks trying to prove something. Trying to prove that whatever human forces come against them, they will hold out, always be there, unchanging.

A motorboat roared by and left us rocking in its swell.

"What a good way," I said, "this would be to get rid of someone. One quick splash. Shouts of horror. How convenient. Happens more than we know."

Lorne laughed, a crazy kind of laugh.

Sean said, "I can give you a phone number, Annie. The organisation has branches everywhere."

"I haven't ever killed anyone," I replied.

Lorne said, "You have a dark view of things, Annie."

I was at the inquest. Playing my role. All in black. The relative. The witness. *I stayed behind that morning. My sister went out with the others. My brother-in-law was distraught.*

We reached the island. Janine and Lorne went off on their own and I dodged about on the rocks avoiding Sean. When Lorne called out, we went down to the beach and climbed back into the canoe and began to paddle slowly and silently back to the cottage.

We hauled the boat up onto the shore, Janine complaining about her wet feet. Greta had made sandwiches for lunch. I ate three. Sean wrapped one up and left, saying he would hitch a ride to the bus station in town. Janine picked up her copy of Maeve Binchy's latest novel and settled back onto the couch. Lorne sat at the table going over his first lecture, the one he gave every year to the new class. He was the magician who would teach them the mysteries of crystal and rock.

That evening as we sat on the deck, me, then Lorne, then Greta, then Janine, the three of us talked of family as we usually did while Janine sullenly watched the colours change. Greta had decided to take a few more days off and Janine said she would be setting off back to the Soo on Monday. It was over. Ended. Like my affection for Lorne.

As I drove past the Fryers' cottage next morning, I saw Harold and Betty taking boxes out of their car. I waved to them but they were too preoccupied to see me. I got back to the city that Sunday evening in time to meet the others in the bar. Tom asked, "So how was cottage country?"

I thought before I answered. Greta had begged me to come up the following weekend. And I'd agreed. I'd had another dream on Saturday night, lying there in that tiny space: Greta and I were sitting on the island, each of us holding a cool drink in a glass the size of a bucket, watching Lorne set out in the canoe alone and paddle towards us with swift, sure strokes. We sat there laughing, wife and sister-in-law, at the panic on his face when water began to gurgle up through a small hole in the skin of the boat. Up and up and up.

Lorne, beloved husband of Greta. Yes I was there. I saw it all. My sister was distraught.

"You know how it is," I replied to Tom. "Family weekend at the cottage. It's murder."

And he laughed. They all laughed.

◆

Two days later, I read in the paper that Betty Fryer had drowned in the lake. She had gone out alone in the canoe. Harold was distraught.

FAMILY

Thanksgiving 1999. They kept talking about the millennium while Eleanor pressed them to eat more turkey. Six of them round the table and only Harry had asked for a second helping. She would be left with the remains to cut up and store in the fridge. Jackson would expect her to make the carcase into stock for soup and, as usual, after a week, she would wrap it in newspaper and throw it out worrying all the while about the starving poor.

"It is not significant," she heard Fiona say.

"I'm not flying."

"We can see that, Jackson."

"Turkeys don't fly."

"What are you saying?"

Eleanor wished she had told them all to eat in a restaurant or stay home but when they'd called a couple of weeks ago, it was only to ask what time she was expecting them and what they should bring. Never a suggestion of them not actually coming or being invited elsewhere. As usual, stupidly, and trying to be pleased that they wanted to come, she'd said, "Just yourselves."

They'd all taken her at her word except dear Jilly who'd brought a jar of her bitter cranberry preserve and made no apology for arriving in paint-stained jeans and a grey sweater that came down to her knees.

Fifteen years was all it had taken to make a tradition. There had been changes. Fiona was alone again. Harry had become younger, his receding hair gave him the look of a worried baby. Was he thinking of those other feasts; the horror at the cottage? He was watching Francie as if there was something he wanted to tell her but didn't know how to begin. Francie, replacement for Betty, helped him to more wine and would soon, noisily, collect plates and take them to the kitchen. Second-wife martyrdom. Eleanor could almost hear Betty's ghostly laughter.

Until Harry had sold the house, 'from under my feet,' Betty had been good company. Then something in her brain switched over to depressed-mode. Tears had become the norm. It was tragic but appropriate that she had died in a lake. Eleanor pictured widening rings on the surface of the water, bubbles rising, and no one there to see. Betty had always brought dessert.

Fiona, holding back time by dyeing her hair the colour of wheat and going to the gym three times a week, was telling Jackson about the disgusting behaviour of some of the men in her office. Any moment now, Jackson would move to the piano and play the romantic songs of mid-century. The lyrics of 2050 as unimaginable as "Hey Jude" had been to their parents.

"It's good to have you all round our table," Jackson said. "Isn't it Elly?"

"Yes, it is."

Fifty Thanksgivings from now, all those gathered round the table would be close to a hundred or dead, except for one. Who would make wreaths then for the door, arrange a centrepiece in gold and orange or bother with an heirloom tablecloth and lace-edged napkins which would later have to be washed carefully and lightly starched?

"Mother," Jilly said in a strange soft voice. "You are staring into space."

I'm staring into the future. And it is robotic, metallic, unfeeling, dangerous and much easier to keep clean.

"There's a full moon tonight," Francie said, brushing crumbs off her blue jacket.

"Too misty to see anything."

"They say it's going to snow."

"It's cold enough."

"It's too early."

"December 31st, make sure you've got plenty of cash."

"That's absolute garbage, Jackson. The world is not going to end because the date changes," Fiona stated. "Wires aren't going to burn up. Planes aren't going to fall into the sea. I'll bet you three hundred dollars that your phone will work and you'll be able to get money from the ATM. Your e-mail server will likely be down because too many dumb people will be trying to send messages that say, Hey, there's nothing wrong. Surprise!"

"Experts are saying there'll be problems."

When you marry young, Eleanor thought, you don't pay attention. You don't ask yourself whether the jokey, tinkering sort of fellow you're in love with will develop into a solemn miserly man who won't pay to have the piano tuned. She should have been warned by her mother's story of father reciting, "'Nay but you, who do not love her, Is she not pure gold, my mistress?'" to her when he was courting, making her think she'd be hearing poetry in her life for ever. But he'd learnt the poem only to impress her and never spoke another word in rhyme or metre for the rest of his life.

In her own wedding pictures, her father looked out at the future with despair: Jackson was not the ideal mate for his lively youngest daughter.

No good to warn Jilly who was waiting for her lover to return from studying coral on the Barrier Reef that her Ted might settle down and let moss grow on his brain. The images haunting Jilly were probably not so much minute forms of plant life as sturdy Australian mermaids in bikinis.

"There is pumpkin pie. With cream."

"Mother's expecting us," Francie said, returning for the vegetable dishes, "for dessert, Harry."

"I don't see my sisters very often."

Fiona, probably ready to snap, *Is that our fault?* kept quiet.

Jackson would later, when they had all gone, make his usual statement that Fiona was right to stay single: No one could live for long with such a dogmatic know-all.

Jilly burst into tears and ran up the stairs.

Harry with a bewildered look that asked, What did I

say?, picked up the platter with the remains of the turkey on it and followed Francie to the kitchen.

"Should you . . . ?" Fiona asked.

"No," Eleanor answered. "Ted's been gone too long, that's all. There's nothing I can say to help."

"She shouldn't be making jam at her age."

"At her age, I was wiping her little bottom, her little chin." *My friends were doing similar things.*

In those days, Fiona had set her own chin towards Bay Street and was adding up figures faster than a calculator.

Jackson began to play "Yellow bird" and would segue any moment into, "Morning has broken."

"The last Thanksgiving in this millennium. My grandfather," he said while he played on softly, "was born in the last century. Queen Victoria was alive then and she was born in the century before."

"She can't have been."

"I meant her mother, her mother was born in seventeen-something."

"Where are you going with this, Jackson? Back to one thousand?"

"I think what I'm saying is that we go on without being aware that we're part of this historical stream. What we've lived through is truly amazing, and at the end of the next century, when Jilly's children are drinking to the twenty-first, they'll look back on this time, the time when their grandparents were alive, with some awe."

"They'll be getting on a bit."

"People will live to a hundred and ten on average. I read it in the paper."

He played several bars of a dark overture warning of dire things to come, of the failure of the gods to prevent destruction.

"For goodness sake, cut that out Jackson. It's Thanksgiving!"

There had never been any suggestion in his younger days that Jackson would turn vague. But we are all a Pandora's box of surprises, Eleanor thought. What did he expect of me? The sylph he married has turned into a hundred-and-sixty pound you're-tall-you-can-carry-it earth mother. And the opera-lover he once was now prefers to listen to old musicals, like a dog whose teeth can no longer manage to chew meat and bones.

Harry came and kissed her.

"Leaving already?"

"In ten minutes or so. Maidie gets frantic."

"So how is it, Harry?" Sibling code for, Are you happy? Is everything all right with Francie? In which was embedded another code, How can you stand her?

"Fine," Harry replied, meaning, you don't know her like I do, she is truly a warm, caring person.

"Francie is lovely. So full of energy." Sisterly reassurance to the boy who had once blown up a frog and then cried with remorse for two days.

Jilly returned, her face a little pink, but smiling.

"Why are you leaving, Uncle Harry? We haven't had our game."

It was a symptom of her loneliness. The game. The simple child's card game, played at every family celebration.

"A quick one," Harry said, kindly giving way where he sensed need.

Eleanor found two packs of playing cards and pushed the cloth back. Harry shuffled the cards and gave a pack to his niece.

Francie called out, "I'm ready, Harry."

"Won't be long."

The cards were going slap, slap on the table as Harry and Jill built up piles of them in numerical order, shouting out "Mine!" from time to time and clawing to grab the stack.

Eleanor waited for Francie to come in and say, "You haven't started that silly game?" But she didn't. Eleanor went to find her. She was leaning against the kitchen counter wiping her eyes. Had Harry driven another woman to endless tears? She dismissed the thought as unfair and went to Francie and put an arm round her shoulders.

It was all too much. Families. Feasts. Always the weak spots were found.

"What's wrong?"

"You have a nice family," Francie said.

Eleanor had heard all about Francie's mother and Francie's mother's young lover. She thought of it on some days with envy.

"You're part of it now."

"I wake in the night."

"It was all cleared up."

"Where there's doubt, crumbs remain. Crumbs of doubt. Neighbours. I want to move."

Moving, for Betty, had been fatal.

Eleanor said, "Francie, listen. I think you imagine

this. It's just unfortunate that you knew him before. She went out in that boat on her own. She was a very sad woman."

"I don't want to be another very sad woman."

"You and Harry are perfect for each other."

"Perfect?"

"You share the same interests."

"You're talking like a magazine quiz."

"Maybe what's important is that you . . . "

"What we both do lately is lie awake nights in our separate beds, thinking about her. She's the other person in the room. Having sex—there's an audience of one."

"Have you seen someone?"

"On the way home from work the other day I saw a woman who looked just like her."

"That's not what I meant."

"And do you know something, something really strange."

"What?"

"She collapsed in the street as if all the air had come out of her. As if, with a sigh, she just passed away."

"For goodness sake!"

"The ambulance came."

"I think you should see that as a kind of end."

Jill was laughing. Harry called out that the game was over and Francie went to fetch their coats.

"You'll take some of the turkey, Fiona?" Eleanor said to her sister. *Father was proud of you. Talked about you all the time. What was I, chopped liver? Was father a feminist?*

"I'll be out of town all next week," Fiona replied. *I*

have an important job. The world will not go round without me there to push it along.

"Nice you could make the time."

"The office is closed for the holiday."

Jackson got up from the piano.

"Any good tips, Francie?"

"Keep away from real estate."

"It's the way of things. Up and down. Houses. The desire of North Americans to live in separate detached units. In Europe people live in apartments. They rent. They don't have this need to possess property. It speaks of a selfish mindset. I've been in apartments over there, that are like little palaces. I tell my history students."

"They'll complain that you're teaching socialism."

"I do my best."

"I'll do Christmas," Fiona said in a totally unexpected way. "And of course you'll all come."

"Well, yes. If you're sure."

"I am capable," Fiona declared.

"I'll bring dessert if you like," Francie said.

Jackson put in, "The important thing is that people are capable of happiness."

Harry started to say, "The circumstances . . . " and then shut up.

Francie finished his sentence, ". . . are not always propitious."

"People don't try."

"For God's sake, Jackson," Fiona said, putting her coat on.

"We are very fortunate people. A family gathered together . . . "

He stopped as if he sensed that Fiona would clobber

him with a phrase, words that would kill any fragmentary sense of occasion that might still linger among them in the hall.

Jilly hugged her mother and whispered in her ear, "I'd stay and help to clear up, Mom, but, you know."

Other people, Eleanor knew, had great festive parties at which the guests turned up in dinner jackets and long gowns and there was conversation about music, about books, about the perfect orchid. But their festivals were repetitions of the same words, the same thoughts even. Jilly, herself, Fiona, Harry, Francie, Jackson, were all longing for the world to start up again on Tuesday when they could return to their work, their real lives, and talk to those other people, the ones who really knew what they were about.

Jackson said, "It's turning to snow."

Eleanor looked out of the window and saw the flakes coming down, big flakes falling slowly, resting on tree branches, on the petals of the last chrysanthemums. For a moment she wanted them all to stay. Driving would be dangerous. None of the right connections had been made. They could wake up tomorrow from their makeshift dreams and over a slow breakfast, move into another level of understanding. They could spend the day being truly a family; laugh and make jokes, play games, sing round the piano. Then she counted up the lies she had told since they arrived. Four. It was too much of a strain to keep on. It was all about pretending after all. They had pretended to want to come. She had pretended to love cooking for them. She couldn't now pretend to want them to stay.

Fiona and Francie were looking at her, waiting for a farewell kiss—or an invitation.

"You'd better set off now," she said and repeated Jackson's words, "it is turning to snow."

He watched them go down the path and asked, "Jilly's leaving too?"

"She has to be up early."

Jilly turned to wave before she got into her car.

She was smiling but it was a brave smile and she drove off back to her apartment where, for all they knew, she might cry herself to sleep. Or perhaps she was going to change into something bright and youthful and go off to a better party at the other end of town.

It was ludicrous, Eleanor thought as she waved back to Jill, to expect that, for your own sake, all your loved ones will make an effort to be pleased with their lives. She only hoped, as they drove away to their various homes, that Harry would tell Francie what was on his mind and that Jill would either buy a ticket to Australia or find the handsome and attentive lover she deserved.

"You can understand a man wanting to keep his daughter inside a ring of fire so that only the best of heroes can get to her," Jackson said slowly, as if he'd read her thoughts.

Eleanor looked at her husband. There were snowflakes on his shoulders. For a strange moment, she saw her own father's face, his wedding-day face, full of doubt and concern, reflected in Jackson's.

"Come on in," she said, taking hold of his hand, "it's cold out here on the step."

HOME REPAIRS

Harold took his coffee outside. It was his fifth of the day and would have to be the last. Caffeine was going to kill him if worry didn't get him first. He set the claw hammer down on the deck and decided to wait for inspiration. He was throwing down a challenge to the world just as once he had gone to church to challenge God. But that was five years ago and God's response had been swift and awful. The world would surely be more benevolent.

The beautiful and the frightening had struck at him that morning with images he couldn't erase from his mind. Maybe he'd stared at them both too long. At any rate, the simian man's ominous aspect had left him with a sense of unease. The look of the young woman with one pearl earring had disturbed him in a different way.

He chose to sit on the bench by the tub of heather, preferring scaly wood to the plastic chairs he'd never liked. Their white upright economical everlastingness oppressed him whenever he looked at them.

Francie, who'd bought the chairs and believed in upright economical durability, had gone downtown to argue with a stockbroker. Her computer, alive and flickering, stayed on, receiving messages from the world and her mother.

A scavenging squirrel ran across the deck.

"Go on," Harry said. "Bury your acorn. How are you going to find it when you need it?" The pitter-patter of the squirrel's claws reminded him that he had a job to do out here. Francie had drawn a line across the two soft planks by the fence because, she said, they harboured something rotten and must be taken up and replaced before the disease spread to the rest of the deck. Beneath the planks was a foot of space and then the cement top of the garage. All kinds of creatures might live beneath his feet, chewing and burrowing and bent on destruction, trying to bring the house down nibble by nibble. But was it fair for a human thousands of times their size to wreck their little homes?

Spare time gave a man time to consider other forms of life.

The girl with the pearl earring, sitting alone at an outdoor table had worn a look of quiet curiosity. More than once he'd caught her glancing at him and had seen something familiar about her and had smiled back in a friendly but non-committal way. For all he knew, he might have sold her parents an insurance policy in the years when that was what he did. Perhaps the company hadn't paid out what was due.

A spider was trying to attach a line to his cap. He moved to one side so that she could fix her web to something more settled. Or should he sit on here and be found years later like that old woman in the story, covered in webs and dead flies? *Harry has found his niche at last.*

With her image so clear in his head, he half expected to see the girl walking up the path to the front door with a crumpled piece of paper in her hand to claim payment on a policy long since expired or to claim him as a relative on her mother's side. Perhaps she'd travelled across the Pacific to avenge her Aunt Betty: The Australian niece none of them had ever met. Or was she a daughter from his one affair come to claim retroactive maintenance? He shuddered as he multiplied dollars by years.

He had at first had an impulse to walk over to her and offer her money so she could buy the other earring until he remembered that the fashion now was to wear only one. Besides, she hadn't appeared to be especially poor. If he had offered her money she might have stood up and slapped his face. Given that he was at the moment a supplicant to the world, he couldn't afford to be named in the newspaper as a sexual predator.

If the girl had cried out, the simian man would've moved in and Harry saw himself returning home with blood on his face, trying to explain to Francie, *I was offering this young woman money and* . . .

Fear stopped many a good deed in its tracks.

The simian man had provoked no generous impulse. He sat there at his table, compressed, the plug in his ear for a radio or a security connection. There was, though, no apparent VIP nearby, no politician wanting to make his pitch to those with nothing better to do in the morning than sit around in a cafe. He was drinking what looked like a litre of coffee from a paper cup and wasn't distracted by the sparrows hopping around him looking for crumbs or by the woman in her electric wheelchair who nearly ran over his feet.

Fiona and Eleanor had played a game called *Consequences* in their teenage years, shutting their brother out; not a boys' game. They still played it but in a different, adult way. The game was in fact early gossip-training. It began with a statement written at the top of a strip of paper. Each player then wrote down the answer to a specific question, folded the paper over to hide what she'd written and passed it on to the next girl. With all the questions answered, the papers were unrolled and the resulting stories read aloud to shrieks of laughter.

The girl with no name
met
Harold Fryer
 at
The Wildberry Cafe
he wore
Slacks and a grey jacket
she wore
A blue scarf, a brownish-yellowish shirt and one pearl earring
he said
Please take this money
she said
What do you think I am!

the world said

Guilty

and the consequence was

He returned home with a black eye and his second wife left him and took the car and all the furniture.

That game was always finite. The players never went on to ask what happened next. Next. Next step in his career. Next move on the chess board of Harold Fryer's life. These were the problems for which he had to find solutions.

"Hey!" he said aloud making the squirrel drop its acorn and run off, "I'm supposed to be emptying my mind so that I'm ready for what the world has to offer." For a moment he pondered the life of the squirrel. Its span, its home, its attitude to its mate. What did its little chattering sounds signify?

Too much spare time could lead to softening of the mind.

There had been music this morning. The usual brand of blended notes had suddenly burst its banks in the cafe as a female vocalist shrieked out, "When love turns to hate," causing several customers to turn sharply. That was when the girl, with one last piercing look at him, had got up and walked away.

The simian man was still sitting there, still hunched over, still intent, when Harry left to come home half an hour later. Was the man waiting for his supplier or a call to say his wife was safely delivered of twins? Or was he listening to some rare music that made him feel handsome and beloved?

Had either of them wondered about him, about why an apparently healthy forty-seven-old was sitting there mid-morning on a fine October day? *All right! I was filling in time till I could go home and pretend to Francie that my day had been useful, that hours had been filled with visits to offices, to 'contacts.'* What he really wanted was to say to her, *I've worked enough, thirty years. Can't I play now? Can't I stay home? Can't I build a castle in the sand?*

Francie would return soon to fill the house with affection and questions. She'd want to know if anyone had called, if he was all right, if he'd put the garbage cans out, if the chicken was in the oven. And was he really going to spend the whole evening watching baseball? Francie was a calm and loving woman. When he'd finally told her, as they drove away from Eleanor's, after Thanksgiving dinner, that he'd been down-sized— a terrible emasculating term—she had told him that everything would be all right. And later that night, she had held him close for a long time.

She would return soon wearing the smile of the successful. Her smart suit in blue and black tweedy stuff proclaimed her as an independent woman who only occasionally had to say to her mother, *It was an accident, Mom. He was inconsolable, guilty, bereft.* And that was true. He might have secretly—the secret kept even from himself—wished it, come near to imagining it, but would never have caused his first wife to drown. Francie had said, *It took him a year to propose to me, Mother!* As if that too was in his favour.

◆

His previous life had been divided into three parts. Life before Betty. Life with Betty. Life after Betty. Memories were slotted into the appropriate sections, filed between invisible separators. Twenty-two years until Betty. Twenty years with Betty. One brief never-revealed affair at about year ten with Joan from the office who had made a sudden move to Calgary. Five years post-Betty whose face appeared to him beneath a watery film occasionally in dreams, and sometimes when he had his arms round Francie.

The first two decades of his life were something of a blur. Street hockey. The yells of "Ca-a-a-r!" Little Colin taking the goal home because they wouldn't let him be goalie. The frog incident, the grade eleven math prize, sex in the basement of the Turners' house. Sometimes the scenes ran together in his mind as if he'd had sex when he was ten and blown up the frog when he was seventeen instead of the other way around. But when he concentrated, drew that particular memory forward, sex with Melody Turner was a stand-out. Rolling Stones in the background, tingling fear of hearing a door open upstairs, the musty smell of a damp Toronto basement, the wonder of finding that he could and that she liked it. And then Melody had gone off to New Guinea and other places to save the world. From what they wrote in the papers about fighting and starvation and disease all over the map, she hadn't done well. All the same, he envied her nobility.

And then there was his professional life. So many doors. So many people. So many repetitions of, Hi! My name is Harold Fryer. After that, years of desk time. Office life, an apparently safe harbour.

Weather to get fired by.

"A temporary downturn, Harold," the big man had said as rain poured in streams down the glass of the seventh-storey window behind his desk. "You've been mixing with the political guys lately. Thinking of standing for office?"

"Every man wants to make one impossible leap, Gordon. One time. One stretching leap into some kind of goddam void."

"Right! We think that in Spring, there'll likely be an upturn and if you haven't found anything, Harold . . . "

To find you have to look.

Last night while Francie was asleep, he'd come out and lain down on the deck to look up at the stars. There they were, light years away, all-seeing, all-knowing, not caring that he, a minute speck, Harold Fryer of no renown, was lying there wondering what the hell he was going to do next. "What are you doing, Harry?" Francie, missing the warmth of his body beside her, had shouted from the upstairs window. Would she come down and lie beside him, make love there in the open, not caring what the stars saw or the neighbours thought?

She'd brought out his old plaid dressing gown and persuaded him to come in for a warm drink as if he'd gone a little mad or was seeking to catch a cold which would lead to pneumonia and then to death. Betty's revenge. Harry's easy way out. He told her he was getting away from a dream of wooden figures on in-line skates swirling around him, and she'd given him a motherly kind of kiss.

Women sometimes understood too much.

And he'd sat here too long. He was supposed to be waiting for a sharp insight, not letting his mind drift aimlessly through time and space.

His sharper sister's words echoed in his ears and still upset him because they weren't true. And they upset him because he knew they shouldn't. It was some slick phrase Fiona had picked out of a slick magazine: "Harry hasn't got the imagination to have a mid-life crisis." Words spoken too loudly at Thanksgiving when the subject had come up among the women and they thought he was out of earshot. Well he would have a mid-life crisis if he liked and wear a goddam label round his neck to proclaim it!

The birds were twittering as if it was past time for them to go somewhere warmer.

He'd waited long enough. He had listened. No answer had come. It was time to get back to the ream of forms on the dining room table. I am applying for a job with your company because. Yes I am/have been/ will be/ good with people. My strengths are. Ask anyone. And they will tell you. And meanwhile, the Party had asked him to do some voluntary canvassing for them.

Before that though, there was this simple chore. Rip up a test piece, Francie had said, maybe a couple of planks. See what's there. He took the claw hammer and pulled out a few nails and ripped at the first soft board so that it splintered and came away easily. He got down on his hands and knees and began to work his way towards the house. He tore up one length of spruce and then another and another. It was the wrong kind of wood for outdoors. The guy who'd built the deck probably didn't know one tree from another. Should've used cedar.

On the cement below there was the nest of a creature which had stored bits of this and that for its comfort or pleasure, a tiny bone, a dried piece of corn cob. Abandoned now, it had once been a desirable family home for rodents.

He moved the plastic chairs and the wooden bench round to the shed at the back of the house and began his work again. Around him was the mushroomy, mulchy smell that meant Fall. He rolled up his sleeves, recalling times in the old backyard. Home. Raking leaves off what seemed like a football field of a lawn. Those years between bits of frog flying into the air and the sweet smell of Melody Turner's skin.

He bent to his work, ripping up another plank and another, glad that he had the strength to pull up and stack the old wood. Some of the pieces were not rotten at all but quite good and could probably be used again. He put the rusted nails in his pocket, liking the clinking sound they made.

He heard a voice. It was his, singing the song his mother had sung on her cheerful days, "Good times are just around the corner." In two months, the calendar would turn and the new year would end with two zeroes. He forecast his own future: The guilt that had remained with him, been buried inside him, would melt like ice in April. A new exciting career would open up before him. He would work and win the world for Francie. With these thoughts, the images of the simian man and the girl with one earring dissolved and held no more menace.

He wiped the sweat off his forehead. There were splinters in his hands and slivers sticking to his slacks. He sang and ripped. Ripped and sang. Some of the planks left jagged edges as they came away from the joists. In no time, he was up to the edge of the house. Standing in the grunge, he felt like a conquering hero.

He looked around him. There was no deck left, only jagged spikes of wood where the boards hadn't come away clean.

Tomorrow he would apply for a job in the lumber yard down the road. A totally different kind of work. He'd be able to make garden swings and birdhouses with the wood he bought on his employee discount. His muscles would regain their strength. He began to pull at the steps to the back door. They came away easily bringing a piece of the door-frame with them.

DOORS

Il faut qu'une porte soit ouverte ou fermée.

—ALFRED DE MUSSET

Twenty-three Divaldo Street was a white clapboard two-storey house set back from the road. Weeds growing up between the flags on the path gave it an unlived-in look. More than likely the occupants wouldn't give a damn about the overpass. Harold knocked on the door. No answer.

He peered in the front window. Through a gap in the drapes he could see a neat room with chairs set back against the wall and, of all things, a coffin lying on top of a long table. *People surely don't do that nowadays!* But there it was, with flowers and a photograph beside it but no candles and no one kneeling on the floor in prayer, no one standing round the shiny box, shoulders drooped in grief.

He walked down the side to the back of the house although good sense and feeling told him not to. Five people were standing on the steps, two odd-looking young guys, two not-so-young women, and a man about his own age wearing a track suit. They stopped talking when they saw him and acted as if they'd been expecting him.

Before he could even say, "Hi!," the younger of the two women, blonde, slim, took hold of his hand and said, "She's in the front room. It was very sudden."

"I'm sorry. You had a coffin ready?" he asked instead of backing politely away or explaining who he was.

The middle-aged man, perhaps the householder, said, "Bring him in, Angela."

Harold let her lead him into the house hardly crediting his own craziness. In the back of his mind he began to tell the story to Jack who would never believe it and to Francie who would. The others followed and the handsome, big woman carefully closed the door after her and remained near it like a bouncer. She was wearing a vivid orange blouse but at least her skirt was black. The two young men sat down on a bench beside the kitchen counter. The man in the tracksuit went to the sink and began to fill a kettle with water.

The walls were painted red and the counter tops were covered in a kind of fur cloth and, no, it wasn't a dream because he was breathing and could smell the mixed odours of sweat and cooking common to most of the houses he'd ever been in.

Angela took his briefcase from him and set it down in the corner, then she took him into the room where the coffin was. When they got inside she closed the door and put her arms round him and kissed him.

"I knew you'd come," she said.

It seemed ungallant to do anything but kiss her back because she was pleasant and her lips tasted of mint. He couldn't help looking over her shoulder at the coffin and wondering who was inside it and whether he was expected to do anything further such as take the coffin away or push Angela onto the floor and make love to her. But the coward in him took over and he said, "I'll just leave you some leaflets. There's a number to call if you have any questions."

She grasped him by the arm and said, "You always were a kidder. Come on now."

"What do you want me to do?"

"What you normally do."

In the kitchen, the big woman was most likely still standing by the back door blocking his escape. He listened for sounds because that was another test of a dream or wakeful state and could hear: Angela breathing heavily; a low keening-like sound from the kitchen; a plane passing overhead.

"It's a sad day," he said, pointing to the coffin.

"It was mercifully quick," Angela asked.

"No suffering?"

"Well of course you knew her better than any of us."

He had a lunatic moment, imagining Betty's whole family, sisters and cousins he'd never known. They'd found him, lured him here to confront him, to make him cry out again, *it was an accident.*

"It was an accident," he said before he could stop himself.

"Oh no. She died of a very sudden heart attack. There was nothing accidental about it. Nothing pre-meditated. I suppose you can't help thinking like that. Given your profession. Being suspicious, I mean."

"Well," he said, "it does go with the territory."

So they knew what he did for a living. Had he briefly lost his mind, disappeared, and come back to be part

195

of a different family? He desperately wanted to see a calendar and know the date.

The big woman came in and he noticed that her lips were the colour of the hibiscus he'd been trying to grow in the front yard for two years.

She opened the lips and said, "We've made tea. You must need some."

"I have to be on my way," Harold said. "I only came to ask for your support."

"She had very little."

"It's not that," he answered.

"You could surely spare a couple of hours. Are people dying like flies?"

"Sheila!" Angela said.

"Not that I know of."

"Well then," Sheila said more kindly, "you just come and sit down and have tea and a piece of caramel cake. It was her favourite."

Her eyes were underlined with brown and the shadow on her lids was green. On this sad day she'd gone out of her way to make herself attractive even though her colours were at odds with each other.

"Are you colour-blind?" he asked without thinking.

"No," she replied but wasn't angry.

Angela was playing with the hair on the back of his neck.

"It's good of you to be so kind to a stranger," he said. In a moment he would tell them the true purpose of his visit and that he had many other calls to make.

"Stranger," he heard the women muttering to each other. "Stranger!"

Some effort had been made in the kitchen. A cloth

had been spread on the counter and it hung down to the floor at one side. There was a large cake in the centre dripping with beige icing. Assorted mugs stood beside a big teapot.

"You will have some?" Angela said.

He realised he was hungry. It was unlikely that he would be offered anything at the other houses on his route. After he'd eaten, he would thank them and tell them who he was and why he'd come to their door in the first place, and leave.

The older man poured the tea and offered him milk from a carton. "We had a silver jug," he said, "but it's in the coffin with her. She wanted it."

"She didn't have to take the spoons too," Sheila muttered with some bitterness.

If they were going to have a family quarrel Harold knew he must leave right away, cake or no cake.

"At least not the forks," Angela said, and offered him one.

The pattern of the fork looked familiar, a scrolly design on the handle like the ones Betty and he had been given when they married. Even the plate with its flowery edge brought a touch of memory with it but he wasn't going to be trapped into a confession. The cake could hardly contain a brain-softening drug although it had the lopsided look of something home-made and the icing was gluey and came up on his fork in long hairy strands.

He glanced at the door but now the two younger men were lounging against it, drinking tea. No one was eating the cake except him.

Angela caught his glance and introduced the men.

"Gary, Ben. You remember Jarvis Gaylord. You met him once up in Muskoka."

As the two of them came towards him, Harold felt relief at knowing who he was supposed to be and also fear that the two of them might attack him if they found out he was someone else. Their silence held a threat which could easily lead to violence. One of them had long, dyed-gold hair, the other an over-cooked afro that was at odds with his unshaven cheeks. They were about twenty-five and looked like members of a 60's rock band who hadn't made it but kept on doing it.

"Pleased to meet you," Harold said, "but I have to tell you . . . "

"I told them you'd want nothing," Angela said.

"Certainly not."

"There. See!" Sheila rounded on the young men as if she'd been waiting for this moment. "I told you so. You can see it in his face."

"They thought, being who you are, that you'd be wanting a share. The house even."

Realising that his role wasn't that of undertaker but that of a relative or close friend, Harold relaxed. He could eat his cake in comfort. If, later, Jarvis Gaylord turned up and made demands, he would be far away. And although it might be unpleasant for these people to find out they'd given cake to a stranger, at least he would have given them a moment or two of relief in their sorrow.

"Well, no. I'm not into real estate," he said.

Gary, the one with gold hair, asked, "So what are you into?"

◆

"You know what he does," the older man, perhaps their father, said.

"Well yes," Harold dared to go on, "it's no secret."

He'd almost finished the cake. Angela was looking at him with a kind of hunger he recognised. He put his plate on the counter and boldly moved towards the door. Doors were two-way affairs. He had come in by that door; he could go out through it. That was a fact of doors. They worked both ways.

"*Au revoir*," he said, to let them think he might come back, as they likely expected, for the funeral.

Ben took hold of his arm and led him to a chair.

"I want to ask you if there's anything for me in it?"

"In what?"

"Your company."

"They're always on the lookout for bright young men. With ideas."

The others laughed. Sheila with a deep throaty chuckle. Angela with a high giggle. The father with a bark that was more like a cough. Ben and Gary hit each other on the shoulder and grinned.

"I'll give you my card," Harold said but remembered what was written on his cards in time to say, "but I left them in my other jacket."

"Well," Angela said, "you wouldn't be expecting to do business at a time like this."

"Give us your phone number," Ben demanded.

"923-4070. Now I have to be on my way."

"Tell him to stay, George," Angela said to the older man. "How many friends did she have?"

"Lovers," George corrected, eyeing Harold up and down.

199

"I don't think . . . "

"You don't have to be shy with us. We're a very free group. Sex after all is just a kind of animal function. Right?"

Sheila was very close and he could smell garlic on her breath, garlic mixed with some sweet scent she was wearing.

"We got some of the old photographs out," she said. "Her at the lake. And there's one of you in the canoe but you had your back to the camera."

It was a nightmare! A weird, twisted nightmare. They were actors hired to torment him. He glanced at the young men and saw a resemblance to all the people he'd ever known in his life.

"I . . . " he began, but they had circled round him.

"Make him stay, Uncle George," Ben begged.

"Jarvis," George said, and Harold was aware that it was a name he could easily respond to. "Jarvis, for my sake. You can tell me things about her that even I didn't know. At a time like this, you can be a great comfort. You go on and get your things from the hotel and stay here with us. We have a couch that pulls out. It's comfortable. I've slept on it myself. There were times when she didn't want me in her bed and it might've been because she was thinking of you."

"Well," Harold murmured, embarrassed and sad because the man was crying. In George's place, given what he figured the situation to be, Harold would have punched Jarvis on the jaw. But he saw his way of escape. "So I'll go get my stuff."

"We'll come with you," Ben said, making a sign to Gary. "Give you a hand."

"I have very little," Harold said, picturing himself making a run for his car and driving like a bat out of hell till he reached home. The rest of the canvassing in this area could wait, maybe forever.

Angela pressed herself against him. "For years I've hoped you'd come back."

Bravely then, Harold said very loudly, "I'm not who you think I am." He thought of going on to say, I'm sorry for disturbing you in your grief, but he'd begun to wonder if maybe the coffin in the next room was full of bottles, marijuana plants, copies of forbidden texts or even guns.

Their reaction to his statement was peculiar. Gary came towards him and put his arm round his shoulders.

"You're one of us," he said.

"Don't be afraid," Sheila put in as if she were going to drill his teeth or shave his head.

"I'm with you," Angela murmured, soft as a kitten. "I'll stay with you. Don't worry about anything at all."

"I am worried," Harold said. "I'm a stranger to you. You let me come into your house. Here you are in mourning for the woman in there and you give me cake and coffee and ask me to stay. I'm leaving now. Jarvis Gaylord is not my name."

"It's all right," George said. "You don't have to pretend. I forgave you a long time ago."

Harold was not going to be drawn into another of their games. "I'm leaving now. And if I were you, I'd be more careful. I could've come in and held you hostage, robbed you, set fire to the place."

They were smiling at each other, accepting his statement without question. Relieved, he made for the door. He was Harold Fryer again, Harry to Francie and his sisters, Harold to the rest of the world. He wanted no other names.

Ben came up to him and kissed him on the lips.

"Three o'clock tomorrow, Jarve," he said. "Church of the Salvation. Aunt Gillian would want you to be there. Stay at the hotel if you want. We understand. You need space. You need time to grieve. And listen, remember I'm a qualified driver, computer technician, salesperson."

Harold's feet were dead weights. They carried him to the door slowly, and he opened it as if it were the door to the vault in a bank. It closed behind him. He was outside it. Ben and Gary and George and Sheila and Angela were all on the other side, maybe in the room with the coffin in it, looking out of the window. He didn't look back but dragged himself to the corner like a man in a dream.

A woman called to him from across the road," I don't like what you stand for."

He called back, "I don't care," and got into his car.

Driving along Gerard Street he felt shaky, like a drunk, and hoped the police wouldn't stop him. He wanted to go home to Francie but was almost afraid to open another door. She would say to him, *You look terrible.* And he would reply, *I'm not myself today*, and fear that it was true.

Francie looked out of the window and saw Harry driving up the drive, the car slowly pushing into the garage, working its way in between the walls, a tight fit, and then the door closing him in. She waited for him to come to her. She sat on the chair in the living room. In a moment, he would come through from the kitchen, kiss her, sit down and say, "Has it been a good day?"

He often spoke sentences and paragraphs without using a personal pronoun, as if he liked to put distance between them.

Now he was standing in the doorway looking at her, waiting for a sign which she didn't know how to give. Finally he said, "A very strange thing happened today."

She said, "You've put the car away."

"Yes?"

"We're going to Mother's this weekend."

"I can't. I have to go to a funeral."

"The corpse wears lipstick?"

"Not the corpse. She, the dead person, has two sisters."

He didn't know what had hit him till much later. The doctor said it must have been a metal object, heavy, solid. A poker, but they had no fireplace. A spear, but they didn't collect ancient weapons. A mystery. He asked who'd brought him to the hospital and the nurse said, "You walked in," as if he were still stunned. Then she added, "Yesterday," as if he'd lost track of time, and handed him a plastic bag containing his wallet and change.

Dazed, he stood outside the Emergency Entrance and wondered which way to go. Francie was obviously angry with him. It had taken her a few days, maybe a week, to get over the matter of the ruined deck. Tight-lipped at first, then philosophical, she had eventually managed to laugh about it. She would get over this too but it might be a good idea to keep out of her way for a few more hours.

He stepped into the taxi at the front of the line and asked the driver to take him to Twenty-three Divaldo Street.

Angela saw him first and called to the others,

"Here's Jarvis. We can start now."

"Where've you been. Look at you. You're a mess."

"Poor thing."

"You can't wear that."

Before he could say no, Ben had led him upstairs and was taking off his shoes and slacks and jacket. The young man helped him into a black suit, too large, and fastened a tie round his neck, tucking his collar over it.

I am being acted upon, Harold thought to himself. They are all actors wearing masks and none of this is true. This isn't my life. I've knocked on many doors. When this one opened, the people knew me, they took me in. They are sure I am another man. Am I sure I'm not that other guy? But if I am, where have I been, and who is Harold Fryer?

"Tell me something," he said to Ben. "If a person has been one thing and a lot of people tell him he's another, who is he?"

Ben was looking him up and down and said," It's not great but it's better than what you had on. And you shouldn't go getting into fights when we're in mourning."

Harold gave up trying to explain as if long ago he'd

204

understood that no one was listening to him and no one ever would. But at the same time it came to him that he must speak out. Like putting one foot in front of the other, he must begin to tell truthful things to these people who had so far done him no harm.

In the doorway big Sheila looked him over and came at him with a hairbrush.

"I'm not going to hit you, silly," she said, "only make you tidy. There."

"I came to your house to ask you about the plans for the new overpass. I'm working for the Liberal candidate," he said.

She brushed his hair gently with the silky brush, tickling the back of his neck, and he laughed. Then she kissed him and pushed him towards the bed but it was only to turn him round and show him what he looked like in the mirror.

She'd brushed his hair forward over the Band-Aid on his head and with that and the suit, he was a stranger to himself. He was smaller than he remembered being, paler, an artefact: Jarvis Gaylord.

Ben was pushing his wallet into the back pocket of the pants and his change into the sides.

"Thank you," Harold said to the new image. "Thank you."

"You can go down now," Sheila told him.

Food had been set out, sandwiches, and raw vegetables arranged on a platter round a dish of beige dip which he hoped was sour cream and onion. A clergyman in a long brown robe was talking softly to George. Gary was dipping his finger into the dish and licking it.

"I want to know what you think about what's going on at Queen's Park," Harold said, hoping to make himself clear at last.

Sheila said, "He's had a nasty knock on the head."

The clergyman came towards him and purred, "I can see you've been in trouble."

Harold backed away. Was it so? Could every damn religious person in the city, the country, the world, see into his soul, see his life, his thoughts, see through his head, his see-through glass head, to the image of Betty setting out on the lake alone in the canoe?

"This is Jarvis. We've been waiting for him," Angela said. "Got in a fight somewhere but he's here now so we can begin."

The clergyman shook hands with him and said, "Bergen's my name."

"Pleased to meet you, Father."

The clergyman turned dark red as if he'd drunk all the communion wine in one go.

"I'm not one of them," he said. "Call me James."

"Don't mind Jarvis," George said. "He's always been a bit of a joker."

Harold apologised and thought, *So I'm a joker. I'm a man who once made love to the woman in the coffin and who has shamelessly turned up to help bury her.* He was surpised at himself.

They gathered round the coffin. Six ribbons were leading from it as if the corpse had flung them out randomly. Six different colours. New since morning or the day before or whenever it was he'd last seen it. Some kind of ritual dance was about to take place. Each person took a ribbon. Only the blue one was left dangling and at a glance from Sheila, he took hold of it. The clergyman was ribbonless.

Could it be that the lucky ribbon was attached to a gift? To the will? To the fingers of the late person?

In his previous life, that is the life he'd led last week or even yesterday, Harold would have demanded an explanation. Jarvis the joker was silent and prepared for anything.

The monkish clergyman spoke, "Our sister, Gillian Mary Barry, departed from us too soon, is gathered to the bosom of the Shepherd. May her ways there be lined with fleece and her sins be forgiven as we forgave her here on earth. Nothing that she did was without meaning and she has left us here bereft but knowing that there is in her passing a gift for each of you, her family and her friend."

On the word *friend*, he glared at Harold as if he would now be called to account for a sinful relationship.

"On the count of three, you will all pull as hard as you can. Please extend your ribbons."

They shuffled back towards the wall holding their purple, green, orange, yellow, blue, and white ribbons to wait for the priest's command.

"If you'd called me anything but June, Mother!" Francie said.

They were sitting on wickerwork chairs on the patio, each of them holding a tall glass of iced tea with a little umbrella perched on the rim.

"June is the best month of the year."

"I'm not a month. I'm a woman."

"I don't know what you've got against it."

"It wouldn't hurt you to call me Francie."

"So where is he?"

"I don't know. He came home and said he had to go out again and I reached for the lamp and tripped. I didn't mean to hurt him. I went to get a cloth and warm water. Came back and he'd gone."

"Well it serves him right, Junie. A man who has lost one wife in suspicious circumstances is just as likely to lose another."

"It was an accident."

"Accidents don't just happen."

"Mom, that is the nature . . ." Francie began and stopped. In all her thirty years she couldn't remember one time when she'd been able to reason with this parent. No amount of complaint during her school years about being called *bug, buggy* and worse had got through to her.

Her mother's vigorous efforts to create harmony through her furniture arrangements and table settings and garden were a kind of retaliation for her failure at the College of Art. She was saying to the world, *See, I am an artist.*

Perhaps, Francie thought, soothing surroundings could prevent physical violence. And if she herself had paid more attention to decor, she might not have lunged at Harry when he came in with lipstick on his cheeks and a look of sexual satisfaction all over his silly face. It was, to be fair, more the face of a man bewildered by recent events than one who had deliberately sinned. Possibly, behind one door, he had found a lonely woman wearing a towel and nothing else.

"What tips have you got for me, Junie?"

"Keep away from gold."

"I know that, honey. I'm looking for short-term, high yield, low risk."

"If I could tell you that, I'd be rich."

"As close as you can get."

"Promo-Fine."

"Make-up!"

"People are tired of reading labels telling them that this or that hasn't been tested on a rabbit or some damn thing" Francie said. "They want what makes them look good even if herds of gophers have been stewed to make it."

"June! I'm green. I'm eco-sensitive."

"Since when, Mom?"

Her mother sank into one of her defensive silences and Francie was left to wonder what stranger had entered her mother's life since the week before. Who had put leaflets through her door and convinced her that small animals were to be protected and cherished? She whose basement contained a squirrel trap, a shotgun, a stuffed pelican? And whose house had contained for the past two years a forty-year-old 'lodger' called Davis.

"If you don't like that then there's a new one on the market. Gerifax. It's going to move slowly but when it takes off there'll be no holding it. It's a small business that produces devices to help communicate with stroke patients. And they're working on something that makes it possible to talk to Alzheimer's victims."

Maidie stood up and walked a few steps, her blue and white skirt whirling round her legs, the straw bonnet tied with matching ribbon. She stooped to pick up the copper watering can and made her way towards the lupins looking like a picture on a Hallmark card. Nothing in the way she walked betrayed her annoyance. There was grace in her movement and gentleness in her profile and voice as she said, "Now just why would I want to invest in that?"

The lupins themselves, thirty of them, nearly even in height were light and dark blue, pink, orange, almost white. Her mother's control of nature was a wonder round the Don Mills streets.

There was no water in the can but Maidie raised her arm and tipped the nozzle over the flower-bed. She held the pose for several seconds. Francie sighed. She despised herself for despising her mother's attitudes. But was it fair for a woman who had been christened May and who had to go through life stuck with her own babyish corruption of it, to call her own daughter June?

"What the fuck, Maidie. What've you done with the friggin' matches?"

Maidie dropped the can and ran towards the house with her arms out.

"For Chrissake, Dave," she shouted. "The neighbours will hear. I'll show you where the matches are."

Harold was beginning to like himself as Jarvis. Jarvis Gaylord was a quite a guy. He'd been this woman's lover and yet they all, the whole family, welcomed him as a friend. How was that for charm! He wondered when they would take the lid off the coffin and whether he would dare to look at the woman inside it. Jarvis, if he had loved her truly, would rush forward and kiss her icy cheek.

Nothing attached to the ribbons could come out unless they did remove the lid. Perhaps they were into some kind of desecration. Were they about to pull fingers or even whole limbs off the deceased? His head began to ache and he wanted to lie down.

Angela nudged him. "This is the best part."

"One," the priest said.

"I can't bring the dead to life," Francie complained.

Maidie had called out, "Come and make the salad, Junie." Junie can make salad out of nothing, she would say proudly as if it was her daughter's best accomplishment and Francie would mutter, I've had lots of practice. The *nothing* on this Saturday comprised half a tired looking Romaine lettuce, two wilted green onions, and a rubbery radish. And as she shook water off the sad vegetables, she knew that her resentment about her name was a cover for something much deeper. 'Why did you call me June?' was simple childspeak for, 'You drove my father away.'

I am standing here, Harold said to himself, holding onto a blue ribbon about two centimetres in width, more the colour of cold lips than of flowers, and I'm surrounded by total strangers who know me as someone else. And I'm not sure at this moment whether I am him or the man I think I was yesterday. These men and women here are certain that I am a man called Gaylord, a man they've only seen from a distance.

The ribbon attached him to them, and fear of the two strong young men kept him from running away down the street and telling passers-by that Satanists were living in their midst.

"A false alarm," the priest said. "Jarvis wasn't quite with us then."

"Ah," Jarvis said, and felt them all staring. Not knowing whether he was meant to be mourning or rejoicing, he stretched his ribbon to the limit again and waited for the signal.

"I realise we make unnatural demands," Maidie said. "It's because we don't see you often. You're something like a stranger but not a stranger and we want you to be happy, to have a good time. But to be with us, if you know what I mean. And if you really want me to call you Francie, I will. But it's not your God-given name."

Francie had stripped the onions of their outer green leaves and peeled most of the red skin from the radishes. The carrot was too limp to be shredded. She looked at it and wondered what had become of Harry. It was unlike him to disappear. Most days, he was either at the end of his cellphone or beside her. Even if he was making that last final push to get a signature when she called him, he would be polite and say, I'll call you back honey, and never through his teeth.

"Was it the onions," Maidie was saying.

Francie wiped her eyes. Yes it was the onions. What

else could it be since life was so pleasing and every aspect of it fulfilling, and everyone around her reasonable and good!

Harold knew exactly why he was staying on with these totally crazed people. For years, going from house to house, moving through open doors into the rooms of strangers, he had seen the same pattern repeated over and over. He could go out and design a room for a particular family and say, here they will put the TV set, here the pictures, here the family photographs, here the magazines and this wall will be coloured dark rose pink because it's the shade of the hour. But in this house, in this small house, number Twenty-three Divaldo Street, there was menace, there was a macabre promise of something out of the ordinary.

George had put the end of the ribbon in his mouth and was chewing it. Angela had twisted hers round her fingers. And Sheila was standing to attention like a soldier. But Ben and Gary were quivering with excitement like children who know there will be a prize.

"Three!"

They pulled. All except Harold who was waiting to hear 'two.' The coffin lid moved slightly to one side.

They gasped but what in Christ could they have expected with all of them pulling! The priest intoned strange words. What demonic ceremony was about to begin? The door was closed. The others had moved closer to the coffin and were almost touching it. He moved in too because whoever Jarvis was would have done what they did. But he wished he was home again, himself, Harold Fryer, successful insurance man, remarried widower in no way responsible for his first wife's death by drowning which had been declared by the authorities to be an accident after a full and fair investigation.

Reverently, the priest lifted the lid. Sheila held up the left hand of the dead woman.

"Jarvis gets the wedding ring."

"Who tied the ribbons on?"

"Not fair."

"You got the engagement ring."

Harold offered the wedding ring to George but George was intent on getting an opal set in silver off the third finger of his dead wife's right hand.

"No," he said. "That's the way it is, Jarvis."

The young men were quarrelling in quiet reverent tones.

"I still say not fair."

"That's childish, Ben. The Reverend handed us the ribbons and he had no idea. Come on now."

"I thought there'd be money."

"Come on!"

"She'd gotten fatter."

"I'm going to need soap here."

"Soap doesn't work on cold flesh."

"Didn't any of you care?" Harold said.

Angela having pulled an emerald ring off the finger of the deceased, ran out of the room. Jarvis pushed the wedding ring on to his third finger, right hand. He could see it was expected. Then he followed Angela and in a moment found himself sitting on the sofa with his arm round her, her head on his shoulder.

"I'm so glad you've come back, Jarvis. Everything will be all right now."

She was admiring her ring. The stone was the size of small pea, set modern style with gold in an s-shape looped round it. Given it was real or why all the fuss, it must be worth a few thousand. He wanted to ask if it was insured. Her hand, ring and all, was resting on his thigh. The Barrys had a different way of mourning from the family funerals he'd known with weeping and prayers and recriminations after the burial. Or as with Aunt Joan, one hell of a party.

It was time to lift Angela's hand off his leg, kiss her lightly as they did in movies, tell her that he was pretty sure he truly was a man called Harold Fryer, and leave.

"Hm," he said. "Angela."

As Jarvis he ventured to say, "Wasn't there a simpler way?"

"It's what Gillian wanted. The way she wanted us to do it. Christmas was a favourite time of hers."

Before he had time to ask what Christmas had to do with it, Sheila swarmed into the room. She pushed them apart and sat between him and Angela.

"And the next thing is. The next thing."

"The next fucking thing is we have to cremate Aunt Gillian," Ben said from the doorway. "She's not being treated with respect."

He pulled up a low chair and sat directly in front of Harold. "Jarve, you know how she was. You knew her when she was relaxed. She said things. She didn't always mean them, did she? I think they've got this all wrong. About the ribbons. I'll bet she's looking down and laughing at us."

Ben and Gary didn't look like such clowns today. They were obviously the sons of sensible Sheila who was a single parent. Angela was sister to Sheila and to the late Gillian, and unattached. George, the widower, appeared to have no other family.

The priest came in and set a card delicately on the bookcase.

"Three o'clock."

George was wearing the opal ring on his little finger and he leaned down and whispered to Harold. "I mean it. I forgive you."

Harold said, "What did you say, George? Say it again, please."

But Angie pulled him away, towards the stairs.

Francie said to her mother through her teeth, "Look. I'm fine. We're fine. He loves me. He'll be back."

"Love!" her mother said and cut a large slice of pie and passed it to her. "Love! What men know about love is this. Cream? They know that there are lonely women out there. Not my one. He's a special baby, aren't you, sweetie? But with most of them, it's a bird in the hand."

Francie mashed the pie down on her plate with her fork and made it into a beige and blue mess. She poured cream on it till it ran over the edges of the plate onto the nice white cloth and her mother burst into tears and the 'special baby' said, "Now look what you've done."

◆

He was making love to Angela on a bed in a small room decorated with pink flowered paper. He was amazed to find himself beneath this woman who was stroking his ears and calling him Jarvis. The pinkness of the room enclosed them. Even if the others had their ears to the keyhole, he had lost any concern for privacy. His amazement turned into a kind of pleasure that was almost solitary. The woman reminded him of her presence and said, "Where are you, Jarve?"

"Here," he answered, "here." And he put his hands on her shoulders and moved them down over her back to her buttocks and thighs. "There."

"Remember what I said, June. He's lost one wife and I wouldn't say he drowned her but . . . "

"Thanks, Mom, it's been lovely."

Francie walked down the path and got into the car.

As she drove she could hear her mother's words behind her like a swarm of pursuing bees: *anyone, married, you, popular, door, first man, down, money, let, tears, daughter, natural, feelings, job like yours, children.*

The door to the chapel was deeply carved and it opened inward. Harold had expected it to open out in a more welcoming way. Inside was a lobby and another set of doors which let out the sound of the organ being played very softly. But there was no organ. The music was coming from wall-speakers. Harold wished at times he'd got into the music business. Not playing or singing but selling it. Just last week he'd had to buy another hundred-unit compact disc holder for Francie. He was working out in his head what this meant in terms of all the music-lovers in the city when it came to him that he was, under a false name, attending the funeral of a complete stranger.

"I have to go," he said.

But Sheila grabbed his arm and said "It's this way."

He thought of writing in the condolence book, *I have been kidnapped*. But who'd believe it?

This is all a dream, he told himself. Dreams like this were called anxiety dreams. The dreamer is trying desperately to get from one place to another and missing the train, the plane, the road. Guilty men have dreams like this.

The clergyman's words reached into Harry's mind like a hand. "Whereas we tend to think of death as the closing of a door when we should think of it rather as an opportunity. And where there is one door there is often another. Has not the Lord himself said that his house has many mansions and do not mansions have many doors?"

Sixth sense was for other people. Francie had never felt it in her life, none of that *déjà vu*, or reading auras. But right now, out of nowhere, it came to her that Harry was in a mess. He had been caught up in something and couldn't find his way out. Instinct made her turn East although home was in more of a Northeast direction. Harry had put his foot in one door too many. Been pulled inside. And was trapped.

"I am coming," she said, and laughed at the way the words came out. HarryharryharryIamcoming.

An hour later she was in a maze of empty streets. There were cars in driveways but not a single figure in a doorway or garden.

She stopped the car and shouted, "Harry!" at the top of her voice.

In Harry's ear, Angela was speaking about inheritance. About the money and how no one had been spoken of more often by her, the deceased Gillian, than her beloved Jarvis. The most precious days in her life had been spent with him. How had he known to turn up on that day? How did he know she was dead? These were the questions all of them were asking, she said. And he could honestly reply that it was a mystery.

"And what will you do now?" Angela asked him.

He moved away from her. In those few moments, he'd realised that the sense of release he was feeling had little to do with post-coital calm. The significance of George Barry's words had just filtered into his mind: It didn't matter who uttered those words or for what reason. Under another name and for a different sin, he had been forgiven. He was free.

"You're out of gas, lady," the dark man said. "Weren't you keeping an eye on the level?"

"My husband usually . . . " she began to say but didn't want to sound deserted or helpless. She also didn't want to say that she had no idea where she was.

The streets all had names like Tuxedo and Branch and Daisy and they coiled round on themselves so that six times she had gone in one end of a street and found herself back where she'd begun. On the dead end before last, there had been people spilling out of a house onto a street, dressed in black, a lighted doorway behind them showing a table laden with food.

She knew that the man looking in at her window sensed all of this. He had a frill of curls and his hands were on the roof of the car as he leaned down to glare at her. His arm with the shirt sleeve rolled up showed a tattoo of an eagle like some kind of gang sign. He was waiting for her to roll the window down further but she wasn't about to do that and have him reach in and unlock the door and drag her out on to the road.

"Well, June."

A common name and probably this man was a good guesser. One time in five he would be right and the woman would get out of her car and be taken off into the forest and raped, later found murdered.

Harold had changed back into his own clothes. He kissed Angela and said he wanted to check that his car wasn't parked in a residents-only space. She followed him out onto the doorstep.

"The stars are coming out," he said, "and it's not even quite dark."

"Darling." She put her hand on his arm. "Come back inside. It's cool out here."

He liked the way she said 'cool,' not cold.

"You go in, tidy the bed, lie on it, my love. I won't be long."

As soon as she had gone indoors, he began to walk softly down the street not daring to look back. Five houses down, he began to run till he got to the car, to where the car had been, to where he thought the car had been. No car. He felt in his pockets. No keys. If they had his keys? They'd stolen his car! He leaned against the wall. A few moments in the fresh air cleared his head. He'd arrived by taxi!

He began to run and kept running, pleased that after making love, he could still move his legs so well. A new kind of guilt was pulling him back towards Angela but he shook it off.

"I will find my way home," he said to himself. "I am not far from home."

Francie would have preferred that this servant of the public called her by her married name but drinking his coffee, sitting in the unmarked police car, she felt friendly towards him and certainly he had asked questions more like a friend than an officer of the law.

"We never had a dog," she found herself saying. "Harold, my husband, doesn't much like them. He wants children and I don't, so we compromise. We don't have either."

"And where's Harry now?"

"On his way home," she said. "They're taking a while."

"The C.A.A?" He laughed. "They won't find us here. I gave them phony co-ordinates."

He had his hand on her thigh and if there was a

prize for stupidity, she was about to win it. Gullibility too. How could she have ignored the clues, his hair, his teeth, his ring? The tattoo! She took his hand gently as if to kiss it and sank her teeth into the soft part of his thumb.

Harry heard a scream. He wasn't sure if it was delight or fear or pain. He knew it wasn't him. His mouth was closed. His legs were stiff and barely moving now. He heard a car door. He moved in the direction of the sound. Shapes in the dusk of a man hitting a woman. His legs gained strength and he went towards the couple.

"Cut that out," he shouted.

"You flooded the carburettor," Harry said. "That was why you stalled."

"How did you know where I was?"

"I always know."

He could live on that for a while. They were only words but sometimes words carried more than their natural weight.

She'd really like a dog, he was thinking. I could cope with a small one. It will be all right now. In my report, I'll say that the occupants of every house on Divaldo Street are communists and will be delighted if the new overpass is built two blocks away.

The facts are these: Betty is gone. I am forgiven. Francie loves me. We'll be fine. The lies I tell about this evening and yesterday will be the last lies I ever tell her. She is lovely, she is kind, and we have a great future together.

"You look different."

"Do I?" he said, and rejoiced. There was possibility in life. He had crossed a line. He'd been captured briefly by aliens and returned to his own planet. He was capable of change. He leaned over and kissed her and the dead woman's wedding ring caught on the steering wheel.

"Francie . . . " he began.

"Just drive, Harry," Francie said.

ABOUT THE AUTHOR

Rachel Wyatt was born in England and moved to Canada with her family in 1957. She is the author of four novels, two works of short fiction, and has written over a hundred radio dramas which have been produced by the CBC and BBC. She served as Director of Writing at the Banff Centre for the Arts from 1991 to 1999. She also writes for television and stage. In 1998, she was honoured by *Chatelaine* and *Canadian Business* as one of Canada's women achievers. She lives with her husband Alan in Victoria, BC.